Johnny Starks Deli Messiah

Andrew Golay

Copyright © 2014 Andrew Golay
All rights reserved.
ISBN-13: 978-1495368059

For Rose, Charlie, and Rick

1.

7:00 - ACCEPTED

The LED display lit up, and so did Johnny's face. As he turned and walked down the linoleum-tiled hall, he removed his coat, unsheathing an orange long-sleeve work shirt, the breast of which bore an embroidered label: 'Come & Buy'—each letter a unique color of the rainbow. His black cap and apron read the same.

"Here we go baby," said Johnny. He strutted down the stairs like a champion fighter and passed a sign that read 'SMILES ARE CONTAGIOUS. IS YOURS WORTH CATCHING?' with a big grin in the middle of it. He matched the expression and then some.

The Produce department lay straight ahead at the bottom of the stairs. To Johnny's right—a vacant Customer Service booth, lottery tickets rolling off the wall, tobacco in abundance.

Moving on.

Johnny adjusted the C&B cap on his head as he passed the organic apple, orange, and grapefruit stand. He made a mental note to check on the yummy fruit later.

He casually looked at the sandwich case. A dozen six inchers of various varieties, a few foot-longs, three pitas, some wraps. A hat poking out just barely above the displays on top of the case.

"Is that you Lily?"

"Johnny! Morning." Lily cleared her throat. "How goes the battle? Up late studying or learning or whatever you do, there, man of mystery?"

"Doing well! How's you today?" He tapped her lightly on the arm and tucked his coat under the counter.

"Good good, had a nice weekend, got to see my kids..." Lily's blond curls sprawled out from under her hat.

"Suh-weet! Nice jewelry—you're fit for a cocktail party, work clothes aside." Johnny reached over to a box of large clear 'latex-free' gloves and picked out two. His huge stature made him almost too tall for deli work, except for the rotisserie chicken oven behind him, next to the fryer machine. He was just the right size for the rotisserie oven. About the same height but more personable. With an easy clean-shaven baby face and a spirit of go-for-it-ness, he snapped the gloves onto his hands.

"Yep," Lily smiled with enjoyment. "We all hung out and sat by my son's pool at his apartment complex, there's a diving board, and some kids were doing flips off it, full ones, right into the water. You should've seen it."

"Wow," said Johnny. "Did you swim?"

"I put on my swimsuit," said Lily, "and I got part of the way in, but I didn't go over my head. Oh, you know what? I did! I took a lap around the pool to show my sons what a frog kick was."

"Froggie kick, eh?" About ten feet to Johnny's left, an old tall guy in a white lab coat was handling some seafood—shrimp, to be exact. "Since when are you a swimmer? That's the kick for the breast stroke."

"Right, Carl, the breast stroke, that's what we were doing!"

"Hmm... I know the froggie kick," said Johnny.

"Frog kick!"

"Right. Frog kick. Why do we keep forgetting?" Johnny smirked at Carl and made a funny face at Lily.

She stuck her tongue out and extended a foot. "I'll frog kick *you*, buddy."

Johnny defended with a judo chop.

While Carl—who had been eyeballing them—looked distracted with manager stuff, Johnny lowered his voice and asked, "Hey Lily, may I... be honest with you about something?"

Johnny gave her a smile and then a tickle from behind, placing a palm on her shoulder.

"Hands off," she said, half-heartedly, and did not move out of the way. In fact, she leaned into his embrace. "Of course you can be honest with me. I hope so!"

"Lily, I have to do something kinda crazy today, for someone—well, with someone."

"As long as you're not doing something 'to' someone. As in, something bad..."

"No! Something very good. Something awesome, that will awaken them to new possibilities in life."

"So what are you telling me for?"

"She's a customer. The lady coming in for a platter today."

"HER! The Drone? She's..."

"Shh!!! Stop gossipping!" he admonished her loudly, smiling as he shooshed her. "It's only 7:12. Too early for that."

"I wasn't..."

The groove of a brand new day burst forth from the flirtatious energy between Lily and Johnny. It connected in their hearts and radiated, energetically stimulating the hearts of those within a thirty-foot radius.

Enough for Carl to growl, "Keep it down over there."

"Quiet," Lily said, and then addressed Johnny. "You want to handle her? Fine by me! Think I want to make a 2-pound platter right now, with the case empty? I have no cold cuts either, so you're gonna need to slice my-an before you do the platter."

"Listen Lily..."

"Yes?" The mom-aged short cutish blond lady looked up and gave her best Vanna White.

"How 'bout this. I cut some for you, some for me. Some for you, some for me. Some for you, some for me. Fayer?"

Lily smiled up at her male Prep Foods partner. "Fayuh."

"So this is between us, right?" Johnny's gaze froze.

Lily's smile fell like a brick. "Of course, sir." Then she stiffened her upper lip and dismissed him with a gloved hand. "Go slice some meat. Thanks buddy. Got all serious there for a second."

2.

Johnny walked down to the slicers. To his left, along the Deli counter, five Hubert brand machines sat, with clean shiny gray blades, waiting in silent expectation for something to sever. One on his right, with cheese residue already encrusting it. Next to the cheese slicer, there were two shelves of every kind of cold cut money can buy. Roast beef, corned beef, Low-sodium turkey, Salsa turkey, BBQ chicken, dozens of varieties of sweet meat.

"What's up Johnny," said Steve, emerging from the small storage closet to the customer's left, the Deli worker's right, when facing the counter. He wore a dark blue work shirt, black apron, black C&B hat, medium blue jeans, and white tennis sneakers. He was about 5'5", and his face, especially his nose and pointy cars gave the impression of swiney confidence.

"Steve! Coming out of the closet?" asked Johnny.

"Steve's coming out of the closet!" yelled Lily.

"Enough of you," snipped Carl from Seafood.

"What're you doing here so early anyway?" asked Lily. "Aren't you supposed to be hung over?"

"From last night?" Carl turned sincere.

"Any night!" Lily was shill and triumphant, despite her miniscule stature.

"What are you two flirting about?" asked Steve as he came around the corner.

"Yo, Steve!" said Carl. "This girl says you're coming out of the closet, but I was telling her that's impossible, you're a closet case and always will be."

"Yep that's the short and skinny of it," said Steve. "But I do have a magic power."

"What's that?" asked Lily, perking up like a schoolgirl.

"I can think any thought I want, in my mind, and really give it my attention, so it's the one thought I'm focusing on, at that time."

Carl smirked and glanced sideways to Lily. He thumbed at Steve. "Too many magic mushies back in the 70's."

Steve smiled. "Maybe. My brain's about as functional as a car from that era. The neurons that are left."

Down the way, by the closet, Johnny stood alone amidst the glory of the Deli. "Cold cuts, just like Mother Nature intended," he said.

Six machines total, ready to slice animal products to perfection. Johnny grabbed a loaf of LOL brand American cheese and got to work.

Forty square pieces in two neat stacks later, he turned off the machine and brought the milky payoff over to Lily.

"I cut the cheese," Johnny said, and then in a mock Asian accent, "Where you want?"

She looked up and batted her eyes with a subtle seductiveness that allowed for plausible deniability. "Just drop it on the counter," she said. Then she added, "Steve. Johnny cut the cheese and it smells funky."

"American?" Johnny said, "should not smell funky. The Asiago I'm about to give you, now *that's* funky." Johnny walked over to Deli land and in under a minute returned to sandwich-chickenville with some nasty, laundry-left-in-the-machine-a-week-too-long cheese. He waved it under Lily's nose.

"Ew, dirty socks!" She squinched her eyebrows and nostrils in one unified expression of disgust.

"Lily, you're 80 years old and you still go out dancing at nightclubs. You can handle a little cheese under your nose," said Carl. "Besides, that's not the first funky thing you've had in your face, I'm sure."

"Oohh," everyone smirked or chuckled, Lily included.

"Hey, you know who Lily reminds me of?" asked Steve.

"Who," replied Johnny.

"Did you ever see the movie *A Streetcar Named Desire*, with Marlon Brando and Vivian Leigh?"

"Oh no," said Lily.

"I have seen that!" said Johnny. "A-hiya, Stell..."

"No, you're not saying I remind you of..."

"Blanche! Blanche Dubois. In the flesh," said Carl, 'introducing' Lily to his sole customer. The lady smiled, looked down at the Seafood case.

"Mmm... fish for breakfast," Carl goaded the woman, and she responded with soccer-mom banter.

Off they skipped into the ancient rite of customer/clerk flirting.

"An-e-way," Lily said calmly, slicing the last of eight foot-long sandwich rolls lengthwise with a serrated knife. "Who all's working today?"

"Trying to change the subject there Blanche?" Johnny replied with a cool smile. "No, A.J. and a new fella are on at 9."

"Is A.J. training him? Look out." Lily smiled as she slapped cheese on the foot-longs laid out on the white plastic 5-ft by 1-ft rectangular cutting board. "More meat, snap snap."

"Oh-kay Ih'll bring you some mo-ore meat," said Johnny in a voice that prompted Lily to ask...

"Is Shigby coming in today?"

"Hold on, I'll cut us some stuff here and then check for ya."

"That's my main man, staying on task. Go Johnny!"

Johnny stepped toward the meat shelf. "Roast-ah-beef." he half said, half sang.

In the store brand variety, a fat multi-pound loaf looking rare and mean greeted him. It had two stowaways: a one-pounder and what looked to be a third of a pound or so, good for a few little slices. He brought the whole roast beef pan over to the rightmost slicer in the Deli—the one next to the closet—and put it down.

The machine started up with a throaty "Whirrrrrrrrrr......"

He positioned his right foot toward the slicer, his left foot back for balance. He picked up a piece of wax paper and put it down on the metal surface below the blade.

"It was nice of the guys last night to leave so many little roast beefs here," he yelled to whomever it might amuse.

Wringing his neck in a circle, he stretched his gloves taut, and picked up the small piece of store brand roast beef. He put it on the slicer, dropped down the guard, and grabbed the handle. With a thrust of his right hand, he moved it forward. His left hand grabbed the piece that came out underneath. He flipped it down onto the wax paper.

Pulling the handle back now, and another slice forward. The second slice fell, and Johnny performed the inversion and gravitational surrender.

A stack of two.

The third slice was just as smooth and fine, as was the fourth, the fifth, the sixth.

At the seventh slice, Johnny was in a comfortable space, but the meat was shredding. Going bezerk. Is there another slice? Will it make it? Is it going to be a pain to clean? What will happen? Only one way to know for sure. Move that puppy back and forth and see what comes out the bottom.

"Got eight slices and change outta that one," said Johnny as pop songs played on the intercom overhead.

He slapped the one-pound loaf onto the metal, and created twenty-four medium-thin slices.

Johnny turned off the machine. Then he grabbed the small slices with his left hand, and stuffed them, hidden, into the middle of the pile of big slices.

He brought the mishmash down to Lily and plopped it in her beef box. "Your pan here is cool enough to keep it tasty, *n'est pas*?"

"Yep, Johnny. I needz turkey."

Johnny looked at her pans of cold cuts, just behind her six-foot-long cutting board. "Okay your highness. I am all over it." Johnny mock smacked Lily upside the head, from enough of a distance that she merely held up a finger.

Johnny went down, banged out two pounds of Hog's Face Oven Roasted turkey breast—"The good stuff"—and made a fast one back to Lily.

"One minute, twelve secs," he said, emphasizing the last word of the sentence.

"Whoa, easy there, buddy," said Lily, save it for your..." she smiled suggestively, "date this afternoon. What time's she coming? One?"

"Something like that. Mmm, yep, one. What else, princess? By the way, you don't look a day over forty-five."

"How'd ya know?" laughed Lily. She looked at her Italian cold cut reserve. "*Mor*-ta-*dell*-a," she said.

"Most rah-*dee*-culous Italian accent ever, but now that you mention it, you need everything for Italians here. I'll hook ya up."

Over by the slicers, where Steve was writing on a clipboard, Johnny checked the Italian pan, next to the roast beef tray. "Gabbygoo!" he shouted, picking up a long, three-inch wide capicola.

"Did you know Rocco's family produces those pigs?" said Steve.

"Really?" replied Johnny in astonishment. "All the way over in Italy? What's the town?"

"It comes from all around the country, where he grew up. Not relegated to one particular town."

"Nice!" Johnny sliced a stack of sweet capicola, medium-thin. The muscles and fat patterns flowing around it made Johnny salivate, looking down at it. He was using the machine to the left of the roast beef slicer, which was now a bloody mess. "Is he coming in today? It's Sunday, huh, so he wouldn't."

"Right—he should be here tomorrow for the new guy though."

After he had assembled three-quarters of a pound of peppered, glazed pig-arm-muscley goodness, he brought it over to Lily and whammed it on the cutting board.

Then it was onto the spicy 'gabygoo.' Atomic orange and just as succulent smelling. He busted off a little less than a pound—the middle of the job interrupted by him stopping, turning off the machine, and peeling back the paper that wrapped the capicola.

"Here ya go," Johnny said to Lily. "Free of choking hazard."

"Heh nice buddy. Got the paper off this time?"

John lowered his voice to 'new Sheriff in town' proportions and spoke. "Are you talkin' to me? You can't be thinking I left on some paper. That is quite laughable. Ha ha."

"No, not you, Johnny, you would never do anything so brazen. You're our hero—the Deli Messiah. Here he comes to save the day! Johnny Starks is on the way!"

"Hahaha. What did you call me, the Deli Messiah?"

"Deli Messiah..." repeated Steve. "Here for the salvation of the meat and cheese?"

"I guess. Lily's telling stories over here." Johnny stood with his feet shoulder-width apart and his beefy arms folded across his chest.

"What do your tattoos mean?" asked Lily.

"I think they mean nothing, yeah pretty sure." said Johnny. "They're tribal. I picked them out when I was younger because I thought they looked cool. You like 'em?"

"Yeah, I always have."

Their eyes met for a split second. "Always?"

They broth broke down in laughter.

"Good for them," said Carl. "They're cracking up. Before you do, why don't you pop a couple spits on the fire, in case a customer wants chicken for brunch." He smiled to his lady, who was milling around, checking labels, sniffing at fishy packages.

She smiled back, placed a card on the counter, and then walked away.

"Hey, if anyone's going to give me orders," said Johnny, "it's this guy." He clapped Steve on the shoulder.

"Oh, hoh, loyalty! A subtle sign of weakness."

"But, though I hate to admit it, Carl, you do have a point. By 7:30, it is important for us to have the chicken on and cookin'."

3.

Johnny walked toward the Deli proper, passing the kosher slicer and its display of meats on his left—but this time he took a right. He brushed the hand washing sink with his left and admired a clean wall-mounted picture of Steve as he entered the Deli back room.

Straight ahead: a sink, full of round plastic containers. To its right was an empty cutting board.

"You changed the salads already, Steve?"

"Yep."

At Johnny's right: a desk and a phone, with a schedule hanging on the wall. And to his left, a human-sized refrigerator.

Johnny checked a couple names. "Yep!" he called to Lily. "Shigby is coming in today."

The back room salad station cutting board, a small one to Johnny's left, was clean. Johnny leaned against it for a second and put his hand to his chin, but quickly unearthed himself and stood upright.

Looking toward the walk in, he saw a cart with he estimated two dozen cooked chickens, ready to be pulled and turned into salad, or alternatively pumped out of the cold Prepared Foods case.

He stepped up to the fridge and pulled the handle of the suction-sealed door. It opened with a *fwoomp*.

Inside: the glory of six spits of Honey Gold flavor with yellow elastic strings holding the legs together and Original rotisserie flavor with green strings.

All six spits were oriented vertically—handles up, on the same rolling plastic tray—three chickens per spit.

Johnny bent his knees a little and his waist less, reached down, and grabbed the gold-stringed spit on the left, closest to him, and the green-stringed spit on the right farthest from him.

With his two hands, he led the spits over the bump separating the cold from the room temp.

When a bit of clear chicken juice splashed onto his black suede sneaker, Johnny smiled and said, "That's fowl."

Johnny spun the tray out to Prep Foods, past Lily, to the rotisserie oven. The stove was equipped with two columns, each with six or seven rows, to hang spits—three or four alternating rows of spits per column.

He unclasped the steel clips on the side, and opened the accordion-style sheet metal, then the hinges holding the front glass in place. He turned on the fires of the two lower burners.

His public watched him load up two spits: Original above and Honey Gold below—both in the top left part of the oven.

"Bada boom, bada bing!" he said, making an eye-popping facial gesture to Lily as he trashed his gloves and donned a new pair. He shut the rotisserie oven in the same fluid movement.

"Johnny, you are smooth," said Lily.

"Why thank ye..." he said, and smiled.

He wheeled the remaining four spits out back and returned them to refrigeration.

"Thanks, guys," he said to the chickens as he went.

He washed his hands and put on new gloves after emerging from the back room.

Then he looked at the Italian meat case and said, "Mort-a-della... Where are ya, morty?"

"We don't got any," said Steve.

"Don't got any!? Oh no!" Though Johnny was being playful, seriousness shadowed his tone. "Are we going to get some?"

"I'm not going to get any, I'm married."

"Hahahahaha. Get some mortadella, ha ha."

"Probably tomorrow."

"Oh, hey, so you met the new guy? His name's Francis?"

"Yes. Weird dude. Super thin, skin whiter than vanilla frosting... The kid doesn't look like he goes out much. He speaks with this high-pitched, whiny voice. He wore sweatpants to the interview. I asked if he had jeans and he said yeah, so we hired him."

The two guys laughed.

"High standards," said Johnny.

"Right? We know what we want in a Deli clown around here."

"Well," Johnny exhaled. "I shall take a trip out back out back, to see what our guy's up to. You know of whom I speak."

"Yep. Keep it on the low," said Steve.

Johnny stepped out through the opening on the corner that served as the division between the Deli and Prepared Foods.

"Grab some pizza dough from the freezer, if the load came in," said Steve as Johnny departed for the supermarket at large.

"Yes sir!" said Johnny. "You need anything from the store, Lily?"

"All good. Oh! May-on-naise."

"Okay I can grab you some. You're out of the big Heckman's containers?"

"Yep, we are. You are too, buddy, if you're making chicken salad, which I'm gonna need some of that, heh, I'm cracking the whip today."

"So you think," muttered Johnny as he walked past Seafood on his left, Produce on his right, and took a dog-leg right through Meat at the back of the store. He waved to the Meat manager and gave a friendly, "Hi Darren." Got a slight nonverbal reciprocation. He kept walking, past the double doors of the Produce back room, on his left.

Keeping it moving by the hot dogs and the bacon on the back wall, the various aisles of the grocery store flying by on his right.

Just before the water bubbler at the restrooms, Johnny turned left. He shoulder-checked a double set of gray plastic doors, which opened into the Grocery back room.

As Johnny went forward, his footsteps echoed.

Silence.

Then, a voice most sonorous. "Johnny. You have come to see Mort."

A white-haired, bearded, skinny man with a conspicuous charm pendant dangling from a thin chain around his neck, gave Johnny a severe, but peace-filled and happy expression from the Grocery office—a small working quarter complete with messy desk, clipboards, pens, and a calculator.

"Creator, you are on point every time. How do you *do* that?"

"It is a gift," said the store Creator. "As is this." He handed Johnny a big 5-lb loaf of Hog's Face mortadella.

"Thank you so kindly, good sir. Is there anything I can do for you?"

The Creator smiled. "Sit and talk. What of the woman, the Drone, who is coming in today? This meat is for her, is it not?"

Johnny sat, in a nearby chair. "Yes, and for Lily. You are perceptive beyond measure. I wish I could get in touch with Caesar, though. He hasn't been in contact during meditation this week."

"Be of good cheer, Johnny. Success is at your fingertips, but your mission hangs in a perilous balance. Controlling your state is of the utmost. Your beliefs are already in place. Do not become flustered. You know what to do. Didn't Caesar warn you that you must complete this task solo?"

"Indeed."

"Truth is relative, fluid, and ascending."

At that time, a store manager (as evidenced by a generic, dress-up business look) came back. Johnny did not recognize him. "Hi S.C." the manager said. "I'm looking for a..."

"Chocolate cream cheese cake." The Creator smiled and brought up the delightful dessert, as if from thin air.

"This guy is the best," said the manager, who then stopped dead. "Wait. He knows about you?"

"You two haven't met?" The Creator raised an eyebrow. "Johnny, Gian. Gian, Johnny." As Johnny rose to shake hands with Gian, there was a sense of balance, that the two men were evenly matched in size and strength.

"Nice to meetcha. Are you a manager at..."

"Billstown."

"Billstown. Huge store, I hear," said Johnny.

"Indeed." Gian took the cake, said, "Gentlemen," and left for the front of the store.

Once the door had swung shut, Johnny asked the Creator, "Do many people know about your powers?"

"Only you and a select few. I blind the eyes even of my closest acquaintances, to each other. The game is intended to be productive, not dissipatory."

"Wow. Well, thanks for the mortadella, my friend. Say, has the Deli freezer load come in?"

"El negativo."

"Thank you."

"Pleasure. Namaste."

"Namaste."

As he returned to the store from the Grocery back room, Johnny almost took a right toward the Deli, but then said, "Mayo" and took a left instead.

He passed a display of Cauldron brand potato chips, must've been a dozen unique flavors, each with its own color of bag.

Then the aisle. Yes. By the ketchup, mustard... "Mayonnaise. Mmm... Heckman's. The other white stuff."

Johnny grabbed two 32-oz plastic jars of Heckman's mayonnaise, clear plastic sides, yellow and light blue label, dark blue hand-sized cap.

He strode to the back of the store and took a left. Passing the bubbler and the Grocery back room. "Will have to write that on the list... know what? I'll do it now." He turned around, and pushed open the Grocery double doors once more.

In the Grocery office, the Creator was sitting in silent stillness. Johnny maneuvered around him and picked up a clipboard. On it was a grid, with things written: 'Pickles, $4.95 LB' and 'Mayo, $3.99 JS' He recognized Lily's and his handwriting.

With a 'Smartie' black felt-tip permanent marker he drew from his pocket, Johnny scrawled 'Mayo, x 2... $7.98 JS.'

He left without verbally acknowledging the Creator. But it was there.

4.

Now back in the store, he walked through the land of fruits and veggies with his trophies. Only the skinny Produce manager was there, frenetically labeling lemons with a pricing gun that clicked out at least two stickers a second.

"Slow down, Brent, you've got all day," said Johnny, stepping up to the midnight-blue-shirted fellow.

"Kinda, regional store managers are supposed to stop by at noon. When are you gonna become a manager, buddy?" asked Brent. "You could be, like nobody's business, kid."

"True, not sure what's stopping me," said Johnny.

"Johnny, what happened, it's almost 8, where's the rest of my slices?" floated a whiny munchkin voice from Prepared Foods.

Grinning at Brent, Johnny said, "At least we found what's stopping me." He yelled to the whiny voice, "Oh, I'll give you a slice. Do we need celery?"

"Nope, got it! I chopped, gosh, it must have been four bunches yesterday."

"On a Saturday?! Where *does* she find the time. Thank you, O industrious one. Wait, you worked on a Saturday?"

"Oh, I chopped 'em Friday, duh."

On his way to Prep Foods, Johnny picked up a fallen Valencia orange, and restored it to its display.

"Let's get you filled with meat here, so I can pull chickens," Johnny said to Lily, placing the two jars of mayo on the sandwich maker cutting board.

"Yep, thanks, Johnny. I need ham, and mortadella, that should do it for now. Oh and if you can grab me those little pre-made chicken salad fake wraps? I'll put 'em out."

"Hey, one thing at a time there, your majesty." Johnny walked over to the Deli and set down the mortadella. He drew a box cutter from his pocket and sliced through the plastic that had been keeping the meat fresh all this time. He cut and removed the wax paper between the plastic and the pepper-infused oversized bologna, and restored the box cutter to its home.

Heaving the loaf over his shoulder, he placed the mortadella on the same slicer he had executed the sweet and hot capicolas. Back and forth, back and forth, until a pile of pink pig patty grew sufficient for Lily's purposes.

"Here ya go, kiddo, some ham comin' up for ya."

"Use Hog's Face! Not the store brand, okay, Johnny?"

"Gotcha!" replied Johnny.

   A short, slowish walking woman, dressed to slice, walked behind the Deli counter.

"Gran! Pulling an 8-to-2?"

The dark-haired older lady smiled up at Johnny.

"Your glasses make you all the more adorable," he said to her.

"I brought in some homemade pasta, you can try," Gran said. She smiled and limped to the Deli back room.

Gran turned to the left and opened a clear plastic container. In it she placed a white fork and loaded it up with little pastas about the size of raviolis, solid all the way through. She stuck it in her mouth, closed her eyes, and chewed.

"Mmm... looks yummy. I'll try! May I?" Johnny picked up another fork that happened to be sitting on the cutting board, and shish-kabobbed a few pasta pieces.

As he savored the potatoey Italian goodness, Johnny "Mmm"ed like a pro. "Gran, you know your way around... whatever this is called."

"Gnocchi."

"Like, the phone company?"

Gran smiled. "'*No* key.' You like?"

"I like. Thank you for sharing," said Johnny.

"You're worth it. Did you do a... chicken song today?"

"Yeah, a brand-new one! I hope I can coerce Lily to sing with me. Or maybe you will?"

"I don't sing," Gran said. "Any platters?"

"Ah," Johnny looked to the side, then back at Gran, "There's one, but I'd better do it. It's a... special occasion, I want to put a personal touch on it."

"Suit yaself," said Gran, and she walked out front to the Deli counter.

"Hi how are you?" said a female voice.

"I'm amazing!" Johnny heard Gran reply.

"Johnny, chop chop!" yelled Lily.

5.

The ham was a quick slicing job. Johnny had it done—two pounds sliced medium-thin and handed off to Lily—in under two minutes.

He looked at the clock. "8:13 and all is well."

He went out back and poked his head against the walk in doors. Dozens of cold rotisserie chickens lay in wait. "Fun fun," he sang.

When he pushed on the right-side door, he felt a soft thud and heard a voice say, "Whoa! I'm here."

And yes, there was Steve, to the right, breaking down boxes and putting them in the leftmost of two big blue dumpsters.

At Johnny's left were high, somewhat unfilled shelves of Hog's Face and store brand chicken, pork products, beefs, and cheeses. Straight ahead was a rack with cheeses and specialty meats open and wrapped in plastic, and farther ahead, a set of shelves with prepared salads and the freezer door on the right. On the other side of where Steve stood, sat palates on the ground, stacked with boxes of Hog's Face turkey breasts, and LOL American cheese.

"Sup, main..." said Johnny. "No one back here but us chickens. Any rotisseries need to go out to the cold case?"

"Some Honey Gold would be good. These lasagnas and quiches and squashes and stuff need to go out too, if you're in the mood," said Steve, pointing to a load on a huge wheeled cart.

"Oh, I'm in the mood," said Johnny. He pushed the load of items out of the walk in, through the Deli back room, and up front to the Prep cold case.

"Lookin' good on the sandwiches, Lily," said Johnny.

"Thank you, bud," said Lily. "I've been at it all morning."

"I know, I know."

Gran was over at the cheese station, next to Sushi. "So the Drone is coming in today," she said.

"Wow she is famous, huh?"

"I get her emails," said Gran.

"So do I," said Lily.

Johnny was checking each container to make sure it was up to date. On those that expired today, he plopped a '$1 Off' sticker.

"What's her appeal?" he asked.

"She wouldn't appeal to you much," said Gran.

Lily smiled. "You gotta understand the women's perspective," she said. "We have been treated like second-class citizens for a long time. We need people to stand up for us."

"Isn't her book called *All Men Are Scum*? How is that standing up for women?"

"She goes a little overboard," said Gran, "But she's so entertaining. It's kinda like those conservative fat guys on the radio. You take what they say with a grain of salt, but as long as they're entertaining, you listen."

"Do you guys think *I'm* scum?" Johnny dated and priced each cold case item with a gun that spat out little blue stickers.

"No!" said both women.

"Phew. That's a start."

6.

After he had stocked the cold case to the brim, Johnny looked over at the vats where soup usually rested. "8:40," he said. "Better put on water."

Out in the Deli back room sink, he half-filled a big bucket. Brought it around to the side of the soup containers—three of them. The signs up from last night read 'New England Clam Chowder,' 'Kale Soup, With Chorizo Sausage,' and 'Alphabet Vegetable Soup.'

He closed the drains and poured a third of the water into each of the metal vats. Cranked the two dials below, up to '8,' then after a pause, down to '7.'

He carried the bucket out back and placed it on a high shelf. The big double-boiler sinks looked clean except the salad trays. Some chunks in the bottom leered up at him, so for good measure, he rinsed it and collected the extra gunk in the drain with his rubber-enclosed fingertips, tossed them in the basket, and walked on.

Now in front of the Deli counter, he had just taken off and chucked his gloves when he was greeted by a strange sight. The skinniest, most two-dimensional young man, if man he could be called. (By appearance, 'worm' would suit more fully.) This slender chap, wearing funny-looking black jeans—as if jeans can be funny, yet this kid's were. Half his orange Come & Buy shirt was tucked in, the other half hung limply by his bony left hand. His hat was crooked and apron untied—straps hanging down almost to his feet.

"You must be the new fellow! I'm Johnny."

The new guy smiled, looked slightly up at Johnny, and said, "Francis."

"Francis, it is a pleasure to meet you. Welcome to the Deli. A.J. is going to be training you today... but I'll be happy to show you around until he gets here. Did you punch in?"

"Yes. Marla showed me how." Francis' eyes bugged out like he was being suffocated.

"Alright, so you are on the clock. Go ahead and get your uniform adjusted and we'll be cookin'. Not literally. I cook stuff over here at Prepared Foods. Maybe you'll end up doing it someday, if you want."

"Is that with the chickens?"

"Yeppers, I do all kinds of chicken. Rotisserie chicken, Chicken Pops, Chix Delish Regular chicken sandwiches, Chix Delish Spicy, buffalo wings, boneless wings, honey barbecue wings, you name it, we make it or get it shipped in. We have three kinds of chicken salad, including one I'm about to get ready to start making. Say, do you know what time it is?"

"Nine o'clock," Lily interrupted. "Hey Johnny, speaking of chicken salad, how are those fake wraps coming? Wanna grab 'em out back for me? Not to nag ya. Who's your friend?" She smiled at Francis.

"This, Lily, is Francis." Johnny stepped back and extended his arms. "And Francis, meet Lily."

Francis waved. Johnny said, "Go on, shake hands," and they did.

"Where ya coming from?" asked Lily.

"Me?" said Francis. "I, uh... I just graduated with a degree in computer science, from New England State... now I'm looking for a job."

"Ah, a smartie pants," said Lily.

Francis gave her a funny look, his body recoiled and then so did hers a bit.

Johnny stammered for something to say and came up with, "Heh, you guys, best buds right off the bat. I like that, how we can all connect and be friends with such diverse backgrounds. You don't have to answer any of her questions, Francis. Come on, let me show you the slicers. I wonder where A.J. is. We have until seven past to punch in, but it's good to get here a little early, before each shift, like you did. You're starting off on the right foot."

Francis smiled at the sincere appreciation.

"Well, let's see here, I can show you a few thangs until A.J. arrives... let me teach you how to be Lily's slave. Every morning she has a list of demands, and she yaps until you meet them. It's great. Now she wants chicken salad wraps. So we'd better get them, or risk hearing her keeping on about it all day. They're back in the walk in. Come on!"

As Johnny led Francis out back, he said, "Here's the sink, it's where we open any drippy meats, like the roast beef or anything that would make a mess. Those knives are super sharp."

Johnny heaved forward the doors to the walk in, moved through, and... "The wraps are on this rolley doohickey here with the other prepared food items. They're made out of town and get shipped in for our convenience. We have four different kinds of wraps: chicken Caesar salad, spinach chicken salad, turkey, and, buffalo chicken. See if you can find two of each variety."

Francis looked and found five wraps. Johnny picked up the other three, and they went out front to satisfy Lily.

"Being of the noble character Lily is, she will fain ask us for anything else this morning."

"Ayyy!"

"A.J!" Johnny greeted his coworker. "Welcome! You have a new friend!"

A.J. looked up. "Marla mentioned I'd be training someone. Where is the pipsqueak?"

Francis squealed and turned away.

"He's joking..." said Johnny.

"So you're my victim," said A.J. "Let me take off my jacket."

A.J., with jet black hair, baggy jeans, and skateboard shoes, stood about five five.

"Nice soul patch," said Johnny, touching his face between the lips and chin.

"Thank you, thank you, been growing it," said A.J. "So, do you have a name, boy?"

"Francis. Is he allowed to talk to me like that?"

"No. Let's raise up the respect bar, A.J.," said Lily.

"Good morning to you too, Blanche." A.J. smiled.

"How'd you know we were talking about that?" But by the time Lily had asked, A.J. was around the corner with his new subordinate.

"I told him to call you that," said Steve, who was wrapping the cheese case. "I'll also tell him to be nicer to newcomers."

"That guy irks me big time. Just not a kind fella," said Lily to Johnny.

"I know what you mean. Kinda wish I was training Francis. He seems alright, despite the invertebrate status."

"The what?"

"The, uh... no backbone. Interesting guy though. Well, at this time of day you know what I like to do." Johnny grinned.

"Play with your chickens."

"That's a-right,"

"Most customers suck," said A.J. to Francis in the background.

"Should I say something to Francis?... 'Unlearn everything A.J. taught you?'"

"Probably," laughed Lily. "Okay go pull your chickens."

"You're pretty bossy today," said Johnny.

"I'm pretty? Thanks!"

"Nice try. Okay yes you are pretty. But you know I think that."

Lily's shoulders dropped and her eyes relaxed.

Johnny continued, "You got my back on a couple Chix jingles later?"

"What's up your sleeve?" asked Lily.

"Hot stuff, that's what," said Johnny. "We got a new one, fresh off the presses. The backup vocals are easy though. Ain't nothin' but some cluckin'."

"Okay. I'm in. Go get 'em."

7.

Johnny whirled and meandered to the walk in. "Chilly in here," he said. Back to an empty cheese cart, where he loaded all two dozen chickens. He brought the full cart out to the Deli back room. Fortunately, the salad cutting board was empty. It would be needed.

"More mayo, perhaps, but we'll cross that bridge when we come to it," said Johnny.

Above the sink: a metal shelf with the soup water bucket, large rubber tubs that could hold about three gallons, clear with burgundy lids, and flatter tubs of the same width and length. Johnny grabbed one of the big size, and a lid to go with.

He wheeled the cart in front of the refrigerator that held the spits of chicken. He snapped his gloves, took two chickens—Original flavor—and put them on the cutting board.

He opened the plastic lids and threw them in the trash.

Ripped the skin off the tops of each chicken. Grabbing the legs with his right hand, he held the body with his left and yanked upward. He left the legs, the spine, and the wings in the black plastic container bottom, and placed it aside.

With the remainder, he grabbed the neck. Held it good, and tore the breast meat clean off, getting all the meat the bird's torso had to offer. Felt it, made sure it was squishy, not at all sharp. "Chicken bones can punch a hole in the esophagus, or worse," he said to a passing Francis. "In case you ever make rotisserie chicken salad."

Francis made a face as if his cheeks were being filled with gas.

"How's your first day going, buddy?" asked Johnny, yanking out a wishbone.

"Good!" said Francis, who stood and fidgeted for a moment, then kept walking.

Moments later, after Johnny had opened the second rotisserie chicken, Francis returned through the walk in with a Hog's Face *Born In The USA* Barbecue chicken breast.

Johnny focused on his chicken pulling. He harvested the second breast, and now the meat of two rested in the tub. He felt them each, with both hands. All clear and safe. Proceed to shred.

Francis took down a forearm-length knife from the magnet rack, and cut open the BBQ chicken. A spray of yellowish fluid gushed out into the sink.

With his fingertips, Johnny pulled apart his first breast—both halves in his hands, tearing it into bite-sized pieces, but not smaller! Most of these chunks were a good cubic centimeter or bigger.

"You just break up the meat into moist flakes," said Johnny.

Francis put up the knife and peered over at the chunks. "Yum," he said with a smile as he threw away the plastic and walked up front.

Johnny made short work of the next chicken, leaving a pile of succulent aerated high-protein base, ready for mayo and celery. But first, about five more chickens to fill this tub.

Johnny took two more off the cart, this time Whiskey flavored rotisserie chicken, and shredded them with the deft strokes of a surgeon.

In fifteen minutes, the tub was seven pulled chickens full. Johnny called around to Lily, "You got some of that may-on-naise?"

"You can have *one* jar," she replied, "before the..."

"Load!" Steve descended on the Deli, wheeling a big metal box-filled cart, as tall as a human.

"Speak of the..."

"Load's in? Alright!" said A.J., taking a break from schooling Francis on the how-to's and how-not-to's of slicing cheese. He glanced over his shoulder. "The load's the part of the job you don't do, because you don't know anything."

Francis looked down at the floor and clenched his face and neck.

"Hey hey, be nice," said Steve to A.J. "Francis knows a lot of cool stuff. What are you into, Francis?"

Francis looked up with an 'Aha!' light bulb gaze. His features softened. "I like computers, and darkness..."

"Darkness?"

"Yeah, I'm not into sunlight."

Silence.

Johnny asked Steve, "Can I bring that out back for you?"

"Got it," said Steve. "Thanks though. I need to take inventory and put stickers on the boxes with the gun. I've been meaning to teach you how to do this."

"Yeah!" Johnny said, "Anytime man."

As Steve brought the cart past, Johnny swiped a precariously oriented box with 'HECKMAN'S' printed on the side. Two jars of white stuff, a couple gallons each.

"Lily, I'm all set on the mayo," Johnny shouted, lifting the Heckman's box over his head like an East Indian woman or Miss America.

"Watch out, you're gonna give yourself a hernia!" said Lily, peeking around the corner in time to behold the spectacle.

"So where's that celery you broke your new nails making?"

"Broke my new nails?"

"Or whatever sacrifice you went through."

"The celery! Sure, I'll fetch it for ya."

"Thanks, Lily."

A minute later, everything was in position. The diced celery, which Johnny drained in the sink; the mayonnaise (Johnny took off the cap and the seal-tight layer of cardboard); and the chicken. Fluffy breast meat pulled apart into mouth-watering fragments.

He tossed in the celery. *Platt*. Then he stuck a rubber spatula into the mayonnaise jar, which he had inverted with his left hand. His spatulaed right spunked gobs of white goo into the tub, until it balanced out the aridity of the white meat.

Mixing the chicken salad now, with both gloved hands.

More mayonnaise. Careful not to contaminate the jar with chicken or celery. Keeping the rubber part of the spatula clean as he mixed the carnivore's ambrosia.

This new wave of mayonnaise got almost all the chicken goopy. There was a dry section toward the bottom of the tub, but Johnny kept mixing with his hands, rather than adding more. He had noticed that some spots were too goopy, and his premonition played out; in the end the entire batch of rotisserie chicken salad was moist but not too wet. And not dry.

"Guys," said Johnny.

Francis and A.J., who had been discussing the finer points of smoked Gouda, poked their heads around the tiled wall and looked.

"Fellas, I need your help testing this chicken salad." Johnny winked at A.J. and smiled at Francis. "Can you help me? We need to taste it, to make sure it's good."

Francis' eyes biggied out.

A.J. held his hand in front of Francis' chest and said, "I'd better try first. Could be a trap." He smiled and reached a gloved finger into the tub. Taking a gumball-sized wad of salad into his mouth, he chewed and closed his eyes. "Mhmmmm..." he said. "Not bad. I like to flake it up so it looks like tuna."

"Okay, you're up, Francis," said Johnny.

Francis stuck the spatula in and scraped out a bit, which he dropped on his glove and ate.

"Mmm!" He gobbled with gusto.

"Better try another one to be sure," Johnny said to him.

One more sample later, Francis was in chicken heaven.

"Save some for the customers!" hollered Lily around the corner. "And I need enough to make sandwiches!"

"You got it!" replied Johnny at equal volume. Then he looked at the clock. "9:45 already? Time is flying! Better get crackin' on the hot case," said Johnny.

"I'll give Lily her chicken salad and fill it up out front," said A.J.

"Thanks, A.J., slap a sticker on that. If you don't mind bringing the leftover mayo out to her too," said Johnny. He cleaned up the rest of the chicken salad mess and dashed out back.

8.

Johnny hadn't paid much attention to the music that had been pouring out of the overhead speaker nonstop all morning. But the fact was, it all sounded the same to him, somewhat. One song now did jump out at him. It sang, "Hey baby, hey, hey... hey bay—*beee*... hey." It sent Johnny into a deep place that happened to be farther than anywhere he had been in a bit. Had he regressed to infancy? Where did he go in that blip? Johnny was not sure, but it was a nice 'working break' to space out and pass a moment. Literally a couple minutes, 'baby'ing on pop tunes.

As he wandered out back, he snatched the empty cart that had held the rotisserie chickens. "Rot chx salad, done."

He passed the meat and all the cool stuff. He was going frozen. Reached for the big cold metal door. **Fwoomp**. Open.

In he went, lugging items—brown bags of frozen foods—onto the cart and listing them along the way. "Chicken Pops. Check. Wing Zingers. Check. Wing Dingers. Check. Buffalo wings. Check."

The cart was full. "Good for now." Johnny exited the freezer and pulled his bounty into cool territory. He **fwomped** the freezer door and pushed *le petit load* across the walk in, toward the Deli back room. Before he got four feet from the entrance, he jumped ahead of the cart and opened the door for himself, acting a gentleman.

In the back room, A.J. was explaining the Deli schedule to Francis. "You should always clock in five minutes early. Don't do what I do. I'm not a good example." He leaned in as if to take Francis and Johnny into his confidence and said in a low tone, "I hate this job."

"Good thing you love the people!" said Johnny. He maneuvered his getup with both hands across the Deli back room, until Lily sprang into the opening that led to the Deli counter. "Johnny, your chickens!"

"Lily, thanks! You are right," said Johnny. He turned to an observing Francis and explained: "My chickens had been in the oven for more than two hours; they are almost definitely over temp. We might need to cool them and use them for salads."

"I see," said Francis.

"Keeping it alive is the vibe that I thrive on," said A.J. "Rhyming is boss. If you rhyme at the Deli, you'll fit in great here."

"Right," said Johnny, "Because we all rhyme." He shook his head and smiled as he spoke. The group dispersing, when Johnny had walked up front, he was looking at two spits of dark and beginning-to-shrivel chickens on flames. Francis had followed him.

"Hey, *I'm* training you," said A.J. as he walked around the corner to Prep Foods.

Johnny opened the oven and took off the top spit—green strings on the greasy legs. "Smells like chicken," he said.

"I don't know if I'd be able to lift one of those," said Francis.

"You can, it's all in the leverage. These big gloves help," said Johnny. He pointed to a pair of black rubber mitts.

"But you won't be doing that..." growled A.J.

Put it down on the flat metal baking sheet next to the fryer, from which Johnny noticed steam or smoke rising. "Did you turn the fryer on, Lily?"

"Yep, I got your back, buddy, I know you have a lot happenin' today, between work and your girlfriend..."

Johnny smiled sheepishly. "Phew, that's a relief. Thanks Lily." Turning to Francis and gesturing toward the spit of chickens he just took down, Johnny said, "These metal doohickeys on the end with two prongs stabbing into the first chicken here, holding the whole shebang together, we call them 'spiders.' There are also spiders between the chickens, and two prongs at the bottom attached to the handle of the spit, to make sure the birds stay put and don't move a muscle, so to speak."

Francis leaned in with his big eyes and looked over the spits.

"Come on," said A.J.

Francis and A.J. returned to the Deli, where Francis said, "Yes sir," to the male member of an elderly married couple eying coleslaw.

With an adjustable pair of metal pliers, Johnny loosened a screw from the first spider, and pulled. As he did, the legs of the end chicken threatened to tear off. He wiggled the end spider, and it gave, leaving the chicken intact.

He plopped the spider into a white six-inch-by-six-inch bucket at the back of the surface he was working on. Heat from the fryer warmed his left arm, and the oven kept the right side of his body toasty.

Carl stepped over and warmed his hands on the rotisserie oven as if by a fireplace. "Hey," he said, "if we're paying for the gas, I'm using it."

"You're not paying for anything, buddy," said Lily.

This prompted Carl to clench a fist and 'air bop' Lily over the head, as if she were a whack-a-mole.

Johnny coaxed the first chicken off the spit, onto the metal baking sheet.

"You're not going to temp those?" asked Carl.

"They've been in for over two hours," said Johnny. "But hey why not. Heh, I probably should've since the new fella was watching."

"Guy's a little..." Carl made a swirling motion with his finger, in the direction of the side of his head. "Eh?"

"Aren't we all?" asked Johnny. He withdrew a meat thermometer from a fluid-filled container, wiped it off with a paper towel, and stuck it in the first chick he took off. He went deep without touching the bone.

"Ain't that the truth," said Carl, laughing and getting back to his crabs. "Right Sushi?"

"Yup" said the authentic Asian sushi maker, in a gargle, with an accompanying head nod.

"Too many scorpion bowls," said Carl. He made a 'drinking' gesture with his right hand.

"A hundred eighty six degrees, I guess they'll be safe to eat." Johnny turned away from Carl and finished stripping the spit. Second spider off, second chicken off. Third spider, third chicken. Leaned the empty spit against the fryer like a bloody sword after a battle.

"Oh snap, I hope we have chicken containers."

"And don't forget to turn the hot case on," said Lily.

"Right! Thanks. I'm doing the extra special jingle with you today."

"How's your platter coming?"

"Don't ask," said Johnny, walking past Lily and giving her a playful elbow. "I'll git R done."

He went around to the hot case and flipped the heating lamps on. He noticed the steaming metal soup vats. "You know," he called to Lily. "We couuuuld make soup today."

"Yeah ha," said Lily, "That'd be nice. Whoops, guess we forgot that one, eh Johnny? Better get those cookin'."

"On it," said Steve. "I saw you getting backed up and took care of it."

"Thanks man." Johnny stepped back, paralyzed for a moment. He then forced a smile onto his face.

"You alright?" asked Lily.

"Yep! Nervous tick. Gotta pack these chickens." Johnny sauntered to Lily's side.

"The last three containers!" Johnny took three rounded black plastic, single-chicken bases from below the counter, where a slew of other plasticwares awaited their fillers.

He also elevated three clear dome lids, which were as tall as a cooked chicken and corresponded to the black container bottoms.

Lastly, he picked up three absorbent pads—black on one side and white on the other.

"Got your diapers?" joked Lily.

"Haaa... No leaks for me," answered Johnny with a soft elbow to Lily's left shoulder.

"Ow-AH!"

"That did not hurt!"

"It's my bum shoulder, that's why I have a doctor's note saying I can't use the slicaz."

"Wouldn't that be your right shoulder? We slice with our right arms."

"I, uh..." Lily smiled at Johnny. "Where'd you go to med school? All I know is what my doctor told me. I know *nothing*! Nothing!"

"You know nothing. Got it," said Johnny. "Your sandwiches await, there, lefty."

Johnny placed the three diapers into the rotisserie chicken container bottoms. Picking up tongs, he three times swiveled and brought a chicken from the metal baking sheet to a container across the red rubber walkway.

He snapped the clear plastic lids into place and made his way to the nearest scale, at his left.

"Multi print," he said, pushing a button. He pressed the digits 6-8-0 in sequence, and the Hubert brand scale's digital display read 'ROT CHX 40 OZ ORIGINAL. ENTER NUMBER OF LABELS.' He hit '3,' then 'ENTER'.

The little printer/scale cleared its throat. *Griiiiiind.* Out spat the first label. Johnny grabbed it with lightning speed and stuck it in place, so that two-thirds was attached to the clear plastic, shrouding the succulent if a bit overcooked meat... and one-third of the sticker, the part with the $6.89 price tag on it, hugged the black bottom of the container. All this he did in a split second, before...

The next sticker came out and Johnny slapped it on.

Then, the third, and it was game over.

In front of the rotisserie oven was the cheese area where Gran had been cutting and weighing creamy gourmet goodies. Now she was over at the specialty display putting out her wares. Behind cheese was a clipboard, with dates, and next to it a few assorted papers. To its right, along the cutting board: the liquid-filled container that Johnny had gotten the thermometer from, and to its right, a Deli clipboard that Johnny picked up at this moment, saying, "186 degrees..." as he marked a few scribbles in black permanent ink.

To the right of the clipboard slot—specific decorative stickers for sandwiches—'ROAST BEEF', 'TUNA', 'CHICKEN SALAD', and green, yellow, and red labels for each flavor of rotisserie chicken. He took three green "Original" flavor labels and stroked them onto his pulls.

Lastly, the cardboard holders with carrying handles. He picked up three from underneath the counter and cradled the packaged chickens.

Off they went to the hot case, all in a row.

Next, Johnny hurried out back to get more black 40 oz chicken containers.

The radio overhead sang, *"Hey yeah baby I miss you because you're gone..."*

Francis was slicing meat for a customer. "Nice job, man," said Johnny as he passed.

In the closet, full of boxes, the music was louder, and—lo! There was A.J., writing with a pen on a piece of lined notebook paper, a huge coffee to his side. He looked up and saw Johnny.

"You'd think they'd make the music more original around here," said A.J.

"Why would you think that?" asked Johnny, reaching over to A.J.'s right, and grabbing a stack of the black plastic chicken bottoms and a handful of clear bubbly tops. "It's a supermarket."

"True."

"Hey Francis is doing good. What are you up to?"

"I'm uh, I guess I should be getting back. I'll be out there in a minute. This place pisses me off, all this *work*." He spewed rather than spoke the final word.

"You okay? If you need someone to talk to, I'm here for ya, A.J."

"Thanks Johnny, that's cool of you. I've been... fighting with my girlfriend. She thinks I should pay rent. Not cool."

"Livin' free's the way to be, huh?"

"Yessah!" A.J.'s smile beamed for the first time that day. His eyes glowed.

"When you smile, man," said Johnny, "You look youthful. At 21 I guess you should, still, though... I'm all man, but you've got an awesome smile."

"At 21 I've punished my body more than most 121 year-olds, and that's saying a lot."

"It sure is, A.J."

Johnny walked back into the Deli and was promptly sprayed by bloody gobs of roast beef.

"Sorry," said Francis, who had not put down the hand guard but placed a beef loaf directly onto the spinning blade.

"No problem, Francis. Make sure you, there you go. You know what you're doing. Safety first."

When Johnny got back out, Steve was putting four spits of chicken on the right side of the rotisserie oven.

"One step ahead of me," said Johnny. He quickly unspitted the three burning Honey Gold chickens, boxed them up, added labels, and put them in the hot case.

Looking over his shoulder, he saw a sight. "Must be ten o'clock."

"This guy never gets old," said A.J., who had come out of the closet. "He doesn't need to."

9.

Enter Shigby Humphalump, Jr. Not an inch over five feet, nor a pound under 300. This guy had whiskers on his whiskers. No beard, just an array of hairs and other irregularities only Shigby could swing.

"Look at those hands," A.J. said. "Pure sausagey grossness!"

"His hands look fine," said Johnny quietly.

Johnny strutted out to the Deli entrance and said, "Hiya Shigby!"

"Oh gosh it's youuu," said the Shigster. His raw ugliness flirted its way into every syllable.

"He wraps time around his little finger, this guy. The walking black hole," said A.J. He then went out back.

Johnny interjected, "Hey Shigby, meet Francis, our new pal. A.J.'s been corrupting his mind."

"Hi!" said Francis.

"What are you, new?" said Shigby, not unfriendlyishly.

"Yep," said Francis.

The two stared at each other silently for about three seconds.

"Welcome aboard." Shigby gave Francis a fishy smile, and then looked at Johnny. "I can tell he's a good guy. Know how I can tell? Heeey! I'm, talking, to you... I can tell he's a good... Francis, right? Because he does... int scare me." Shigby smiled as if waiting for a round of applause after his soliloquy.

"Well, glad that wasn't awkward! You two are going to be like peas in a pod, I can tell right off the bat."

"A.J hasn't been, around much, this morning." said Francis. "And when he is, he yells at me or tells me what I can't do."

"That's probably for the best, you shouldn't listen to him," croaked Shigby. "I-ull train you."

"Train him to munch?" said Johnny.

Shigby smiled. "Ha ha, you're more of a muncher than I am, and you know it, Johnny."

"I AM? When do I ever much?"

"You eat the shavings off the roast beef. Don't eeeven lie about it."

"Shigby, come on now... not in front of the new chap..."

"You brought up the munchin'! Can I help you?"

Shigby look out at the counter, to a young, blonde attractive female. The way she carried herself screamed 'High Value!'. "Yes, may I please have a... gosh, I hardly ever go to the deli..."

"We don't see too many people like yoooouuu here," said Shigby. "Maybe that's how you stay look-ing like thaaaat."

"Looking like what?"

"This is how *not* to talk to a customer," sidespoke Johnny to a bemused Francis.

"Like, pretty."

"Aww..." the girl smiled. "You are adorable. What's your name?"

"Shigby."

"Well, Shigby, I'll have half a pound of low-sodium American cheese, medium sliced, please."

"You got it." Shigby waddled out back, his khakis fitting loose but staying up... his shirt not really tucked in but whatever. It's Shigby.

Francis asked Johnny, "Is Shigby a guy or a girl?"

"Seriously?" asked Johnny.

"Guy?"

"Yeah, he's a guy. There was some talk about him having had a... Hey there how are you today!"

"Good," said a bald gentleman with tufts of gray hair on the sides of his head. He wore a black corduroy sports coat, and a black-and-white checkered button-down shirt underneath. He looked to his left at the young lady, extended his arm and said, "Are you next, miss?"

She smiled toward him. "I'm being helped, thanks."

"You are welcome. Let's see..." he unglued his eyes from her, and stared ahead at Johnny and the boards with prices overhead. "Many choices, many sales... What do you recommend?"

"Well," said Johnny. "What do you like? What's your flavor?"

"Beef."

"Ho-keh, we have on saaaallleeee... the Hog's Face roast beef for $9.99 a pound."

"Whoa!" the fella looked to the girl for a reaction. She fluffed her hair but did not turn in his direction. "What's the usual price?"

"Twelve ninety nine a pound. And yes, it's *that* good."

"I just need something simple for sandwiches, doesn't hafta to be too fancy. How about that red pastrami?"

"Good choice. It rings in at $5.99 a pound and gets rave reviews. I like it, myself, with mayonnaise."

"Yum. I'll take half a pound."

"You got it."

Shigby had returned and cut a slice of the cheese. He turned around and showed it to the girl, "How's this?"

"Good I guess!" She smiled earnestly.

"Would you like to try a slice?"

"No, it's not for me." The blonde tucked a lock of hair behind her ear.

Johnny shifted the plastic handle of the window below the counter. Through the newly-formed opening, he reached his hand and picked up a pair of tongs. He scooped what would be about two handfuls.

"Slow day, today," he said.

"It's a Sunday in Summer... people are on vacation," said his customer.

"And there was the big basketball game last night. Everyone must've slept in."

With his right hand, he grabbed a plastic bag from the flat metal area below the counter, and opened it to receive the pastrami.

He lifted it onto the scale. "It's a little under. Want me to top it off?"

"That's good, thanks," said the guy.

Shigby weighed, bagged, and tagged his customer's order, and handed it to her. "Something else?"

"No thanks! Have a good one. And thank you for the compliment." She gave him a little wave as she walked off.

Shigby waved.

"I think she likes you," said Johnny's customer to Shigby.

Shigby waited a few moments and replied, "You didn't need to say that."

"Now Shigby, be nice to the gentleman..."

"No, he's right," said the guy. "Though trying to be cutesy, I was out of line. Thank you. Shigby's your name? Highest regards."

Johnny and Francis shared a fun moment of grinning eye contact, at Shigby's recent accolades.

Johnny handed the pastrami to his customer. "Something else, today?"

"That'll be all, thanks," said the gent. He smiled. "Have a good one."

The coast clear, "Hey," said Johnny. "Do you guys know how to hypnotize someone when you're talking to them?"

"How?" asked Francis, all ears.

"You stand how they are standing, as if you are a mirror image. Match their voice tone, so if they're talking low, you talk low—though not the exact same or else they'll think you're making fun of them. And so on. You can play around with it. And then you can throw in embedded commands. Check this out. Hey Lily," said Johnny.

Lily turned around, her hands by her sides, and said, "Yo."

"Gangsta," he said, dropping his hands down. "I was outside, feeling a *touch* of the sniffles, and I saw *your* car. I thought, now there's a girl who uses her *head*, to get such a nice car." On each emphasized word, he deepened his voice a shade.

Lily touched her head.

"HA! See what I did there?" asked Johnny.

Francis clapped. "Bravo!"

Shigby shook his head and put his hand on his hip.

"What!?" said Lily.

"I just made you touch your head."

"No you didn't. How could you?"

"Listen again. I was outside, feeling a *touch* of the sniffles, and I saw *your* car. I thought, now there's a girl who uses her *head*, to get such a nice car." Johnny dropped his voice to a noticeable depth on the words 'touch,' 'your,' and 'head.'

"OH! You... How did you..."

"Magic. Guys. Use these newfound powers only for good."

Francis pranced to the counter. "Hello, can I help you?"

The customer seemed unremarkable at first glance. A few wrinkles, the distant look for something just out of reach. Maybe that Thanksgiving when the turkey got up on the table and danced. He chomped his fleshy jaws and put his varicose hands on the counter.

"Young man, I'll have half a pound of liverwurst."

"Yes, sir." Francis fairly flitted to the rear cooler entry. On the door windows, someone had drawn a smile in the condensation with a fist. Drops from the eyes dripped down—three streaks per.

Once he was at the cheese and specialty rack, he searched frantically. "Liverwurst, liverwurst."

"Liverwust? Regular or low-sodium." Steve turned his head and body to address Francis.

Francis craned his neck to his left, as if to telepathically send furtive requests or simply nasty looks to the customer.

"Should I ask?"

"Plain liverwurst is this one. You can bring them both out and give the customer a choice, if you like. Either way. They probably want regular though, if they didn't say otherwise."

"Hmm." Francis picked up both foot long, three-inch diameter squishy pink loaves, and made his way out to the counter. Opening the door with his back, and swiveling out in a sweeping move, he let his fangs show and his arms extend—and he asked, "Regular or low sodium?"

"Regular, thank you," said the man.

"Okay!"

Francis brought both loaves out to a slicer and put the low sodium one down.

"So far so good," said the old codger.

Francis blushed and said, "Heh, ah, how, would you like it sliced?"

"Oh, pretty thick, about a quarter inch." The man smiled, baring drippy gums.

"Al-rite!" Francis said with an upward inclination. He unwrapped the regular liverwurst and set it on the machine. Placing the guard in position, he turned on the motor, adjusted the thickness to 3, and...

First slice. Picked it up and showed the man. "How's that?"

"Little thickah."

"K!" Francis set the knob between 3 and 4, and sliced.

"Like this?"

"Yeah! Mmm, that's good. We'll keep the first slice."

"Can't let it go to waste!"

"Right kid. That's half a pound."

Half a pound later, the man and Francis were beaming, and moving separate ways. Francis back to the cooler to put away the liverwurst—after he had wrapped it up—and the fella to the rest of the store.

"Nice job, Francis!" called an observant Johnny, who was putting out Heckman's ketchup & mayonnaise packets and Hog's Face Deli-Style and Honey mustard. "You're not even going to need a trainer soon. Hey where's A.J.?"

"He said he was taking a break, but that was a while ago."

"That guy," said Johnny.

10.

At 10:25, Johnny visited the fryer. Watered his gloves by gripping a nearby damp towel, and flicked a drop into the oil. It sizzled and burst.

He poured a bag of Chicken Pops into the basket. Some crumbs flaked into the lipid liquid and caused a sizzle. Johnny stopped after about two-thirds was in, and placed the bag on the cart with one hand while he dropped in the chicken.

It went up with a *fwoosh* as grease met frozen water around and within the chicken flesh.

He pressed the third button on the front panel of the fryer. The red numbers lit up: 2:45 and ticking.

In that two minutes and forty five seconds, Johnny...

Turned around and looked down under the counter. "Chicken Pops containers... Chicken Pops containers... Doh! Better check out back."

"Need lids too, or just the bottoms?"

"That is an excellent question." Johnny took a peek down below, grabbed a tower of three-inch bubble lids, and put it up top. "Just the bottoms. You got my back though, thanks. Ready to learn the new song? Yep? I'll teach it to you when I return." With that Johnny skittled to the closet.

The boxes in the closet were piled high and wide—the width of six men and the height of a full-statured person.

Johnny found a stack of cardboard cups that looked like they could be small popcorn holders. He had grabbed them and turned around, when he noticed a sheet of paper with the words *'Kill 'Em All'* in black.

"A.J...." Johnny shook his head and kept walking.

As he rounded the corner to Prep Foods, the fryer told him he had one minute remaining. With a felt-tip marker, he wrote '11:00' on the bottoms of eight cups.

"Didja mark the Chicken Pops a half hour up? Marla was buggin' me about changing them more often," probed Lily.

"Yep, I did," said Johnny. As soon as he had marked the last one, *BEEP! BEEP! BEEP!* Off went the buzzer. The fryer had finished its work. Johnny pulled the basket up out of the grease to see an array of golden brown, crisp little nuggets of fleshy delight.

He shook the payload like a maraca, and a flurry of excess oil drifted down into the vat.

He dumped the Chicken Pops into a rectangular black plastic pan, which had a paper towel folded in the bottom of it. Restoring the basket to its home position, he picked up the black pan and shook it. Some of the Chicken Pops looked dryer; most remained all greased up.

Johnny swiveled around and placed the pan of Chicken Pops on the counter. Dipping one of the circular cardboard containers into the pan, he filled each of the other seven in series, and with the leftover Pops, filled the scooper. "Perfecto."

"So, how about that song?" asked Lily.

"Right." Johnny popped a bubble lid onto each container, brought four over to the hot case, came back, and brought the other four.

As he opened a bag of Wing Zingers, he sang:

*"Now's the time to
Stop by the Deli, and
Get your Chix Delish
Chicken Sandwich, the
Only thing that beats the
Taste is the price get the
Chix (Ba-GAWK! Ba-GAWK!) That's your wish! (Ba-GAWK! Ba-GAWK!)"*

The melody followed an ascending scale, with an arching pattern: walk two steps up, then jump a third down... repeat starting the next step up in the scale. The last "Chix" was on the seventh, and the "Wish!" brings us back to *do*.

"Whatcha think?"

"You want me to do the '*ba-gawk! ba-gawk!'* right?"

"That's a-right..."

"Okay, you're on, bucko. Let's get those Chix Delish made so we can do it. Heh heh that sounded a little naughty. Johnny, that's a good song. You got me all riled up."

Johnny dumped out a partial bag of Wing Zingers and filled most of a fryer basket. "I got another one if we can do it later."

He pressed a button, and the timer lit up the display—'5:00.' It began counting down, and as Johnny lowered the basket into the oil, the whole affair got loud.

Johnny reached underneath his station and grabbed orange and white striped paper bags. On each, he marked, 'Wing Zingers.'

"How's your sandwichies coming?" asked Johnny.

"Are you kiddin' me? I've filled the case twice already, and it's not even 11. Not even quarter of!"

"Funny, the Deli itself has been slow. Big on-the-go brunch crowd today."

"You never can tell... they must like what I'm putting out."

"That's true. Are you taking your break at 11?"

Lily arranged on a tray five wraps, enclosed in plastic and stickered up, ready to serve. She wiped down her cutting board. "That *is* the plan. Gran, you getting ready for a break?"

"Yep."

"Will you sing a jingle with me before you go?" asked Johnny.

"Sure, if you get the Chix Delishes done on time," said Lily. "Of course I will."

"Alrighty."

A.J. came around the corner. "Do you guys think it's better to be mediocre at your own life purpose, or excellent at someone else's?"

"Aren't you supposed to be training someone?" asked Lily, with a sharp voice.

"Yes?" said A.J. "I dunno. I guess so. Hey dig this rap. *When you got it going on, you hit it. Get it like you own the bone. There is nothing you can't do because you are you. You are the one. You are the way. You are the brightest shining day. You are the surge. You are the purge. You are the one who does not need words, girl i adore your shore because you are the one who i know i can turn to when i just want to be who i am there's no need to hide we are to abide in the vibe for ever and ever and ever...*"

"Hey A.J.," said Steve, who had been showing Francis how to refill sanitation fluid bottles. "Don't just do something... stand there!"

"You got it, Steve. Dibs on chicken salad." A.J. looked at Johnny with expectation, as if ready to defend a disagreement.

"Go for it," said Johnny, dumping out the Wing Zingers into a different black plastic pan than the one in which he had drained the Chicken Pops. "You know I just made some? You ate half of it, remember?"

"Ha ha. We *will* need more later."

"Don't be pulling it into tiny little pieces," said Lily.

Johnny filled the fryer basket halfway with Wing Dingers and dropped it like it was frozen.

"Five minutes," he said, as he portioned the Wing Zingers into paper bags, four to six wings a bag. Labels on with a *bzzzz/slap!*

Into the hot case they went, next to the Chicken Pops.

"Fried chicken! Can't forget that." said Johnny. He tromped back to the freezer and fetched a big box of frozen fowl.

When he returned, two minutes were left on the Wing Dingers. "Time flies," he announced, then asking Lily, "What do you think about mind control, and seduction?"

"That's quite a conversation topic, way to start your work week!" she said as she pretended to work her butt off. She leaned in. "A.J.'s rap was pretty positive, don't you think? Even if it was weird... maybe there's more to him."

"Well, Sunday, yeah I guess that's the start of the week. An-e-way... for example. In cults, followers worship the leader, and ascribe to them powers of deities. But why? Because of the image they put out, right?"

"Right... or maybe something deeper. Hey, I thought you were making Chix next, buddy."

"Something deeper," said Johnny. "Good point. Any idea what that 'deeper something' might be?"

"Charisma! People power."

"Right. And I know, from interacting with you, that you value charisma, even in the little things."

"You noticed! What was it, my earrings?"

"No." Johnny paused. "It was..."

The fryer beeped. Johnny pushed the button and dumped the Dingers.

"The way you are. Customers light up when they see you. You have fans, rather than customers. Know what I mean?"

"Oh Johnny, stop it," Lily laughed.

"What if you could use the rapport you build with people... to change them."

"What?"

"In a good way." Johnny moved the Wing Dingers over to the counter, bagged and tagged 'em. "We always say, 'Have a good day.' Well, what if you could *make* your customers have a good day. Permanently." Dingers in the hot case.

A.J. approached with a non sequitur in his mouth.

"When you get to the point of having everything and nothing at the same time, what do you do?"

Lily furrowed her brow and looked as if to cast an 'A.J. begone' spell.

Johnny busted out both baskets and filled them to the brim with fried chicken, one thigh for every drumstick and wing and breast. He dropped them into the oil and closed the fryer lid, which had the effect of sealing it and turning it into a giant pressure cooker. He set the timer for fifteen minutes.

"When you open up the doors of communication, it's all over," said A.J. "You get in the zone and there's no turning back." Then he whispered in Johnny's ear, "Dude I am trippin' FACE!"

Blanched looked over and gave a rye (sic) smile. "Don't just do something, stand there!" she hollered.

A.J: "We heard that one the last time Steve said it, twenty minutes ago, but thanks for reminding us, Blanche!"

"That was funny two hours ago," Johnny informed his intoxicated coworker. "Francis looks like he could use a hand, though."

Francis was wrestling the plastic off a sharp cheddar. The plastic was winning.

A.J. left to scold his assistant.

Johnny said, "Ah, I can't believe I forgot to do the Chix Delish before the fried chicken. I am sorry. I honestly did not mean to. Want to take your break now?"

"No, it's okay, right, Gran? Want to go in 20?"

Gran looked up from arranging a tray of crumbled Gorgonzola packages. "For the chicken song? Sure."

Johnny went underneath the counter and emerged with an 8-piece box, and two 4-piece boxes. "That should be good for starters."

He shook the extra oil off the chicken and dumped it into a black full-size pan to the right of the fryer. He moved the pan over to the Prep counter and, with tongs, put the chicken in the boxes.

"Forgot the wax paper," said Lily.

"What would I do without ya," said Johnny.

"You'd sing your chicken song by yourself!"

"Alright, already. Ten minutes, if you can endure it."

"No prob."

Johnny dropped six Regular Chix Delish into the fryer and set the timer for 5.

He put a half-sheet of wax paper in the bottom of each fried chicken box. Dropped in the chicken, which maintained its greasiness that much more. Three tags and three labels later, the fried chicken was in the hot case.

"Do we have buns?" asked Johnny, turning to look below and to the left of the fryer, under the pan where he had dumped the fried chicken.

"I got buns," said Lily, slapping some tuna onto croissants.

"Yeah you do," said Johnny, venturing a peek at her hindquarters.

"Take it easy," said Lily, smiling.

Johnny moved a bag of hamburger buns onto his cutting board. He took out ten and lined them up, split, in two rows, top and bottom.

He shifted to the left, reached below, and said, "Watch ya knees."

With that, he opened the fridge below Lily's station. Pickles in jars, servings of mayonnaise in plastic containers, various sauces and condiments, and... "Butter Buds. Yummy. I *can* believe it's not butter."

"We got a believer," said Lily as Johnny closed the fridge and went to the buns.

The Butter Buds bottle was plastic with a spray top. He gave each bun, top and bottom, a little squirt.

At the scale, he typed the number 255. The screen read 'CHIX DELISH REG'.

He hit the QTY button and then the number 6. At that time, the fryer went off.

He pushed the fryer button, pulled up the Chix, and then turned back to the scale. He hit PRINT, slapped three labels on his left shirt sleeve, and three on his right, as they scrolled out on autopilot.

Johnny dumped the Regular Chix to the side and dropped four Spicys. He then slid the meat between each of the six buns.

Reaching below, his hand hit cold steel.

"Oh no!" he said. "No bags!"

"Uh oh," said Lily.

"I'll run and grab 'em," said Johnny.

Before Lily could say, "K!" Johnny had gone to the freezer and was back, Regular and Spicy Chix Delish bags in hand.

"You are fast, dude!" said Lily.

Johnny put the bags on top of the rotisserie oven for a few seconds. Once they were thawed, he bagged and tagged the six Chix, stuck them in a sandwich rack, and the hot case just got a little more Chickeny.

Four Spicy Chix labels later, four bags thawed on the counter, and the beeper went off again. This time, Johnny was ready. He slammed those puppies in, bagged, tagged, signed, sealed, delivered.

"You ready to sing, kiddo?"

"Let's do it."

Johnny and Lily marched to the Deli back room, where Gran was spraying off the salad trays Steve had changed earlier.

"You are the best, Gran," said Johnny.

"Unlike A.J." she replied with a scowl. "He's been hiding out all morning. And the way he's been training that poor new fellow... disgraceful."

After a silence, Johnny said, "Yeah! Sure is."

"Okay I gotta get a break in here, my main man. C'mon."

"Let's practice one time."

They did.

"And away we go."

Johnny picked up the phone, pressed INTERCOM, and woke up the store.

"Ba-GAAAWWWKK!

"Now's the time to

Stop by the Deli, and
Get your Chix Delish
Chicken Sandwich, the
Only thing that beats the
Taste is the price get the
Chix"

Lily: *"(Ba-GAWK! Ba-GAWK!)"*

Johnny: *"That's your wish!"*

Lily: *"Ba-GAWK! Ba-GAWK!"*

A few customers applauded, and Gran said, "That was awesome!"

As Johnny and Lily re-emerged into Prep Foods, Carl was ready with a shaking head and a scowl.

"You're just jealous," said Johnny.

Carl laughed. "Oh yeah. So jealous."

Sushi laughed.

"Too many mai-tais," said Carl, pointing at Johnny and Lily.

Sushi laughed harder.

"Break!" said Lily. "You mind putting out more fake wraps for me?" Lily batted her eyelashes toward Johnny and gave him an innocent smile.

"When you put it like that, sure," said Johnny. He patted her bum shoulder.

Gran emerged from the back room, slinging an overarm tote bag. The girls walked out together, toward the front of the store. "Cya in fifteen!"

11.

A portly salmon-lipped customer stepped up to the plate. Standing, hands out of pockets, flat and loose. Baggy tan denim jacket.

"Hi!" said Johnny, all friendly like.

In the dish atop the Deli counter, three half-sour pickles felt baritone vibrations as the man said, "May i have, a half a pound of Buck Wild buffalo chicken? Thanks." His eyes smiled a bit, as...

Johnny replied, "Sure thang!" He turned and stooped to grab the chicken.

He picked it up with his right hand, whose gloves instantly turned a blazing orange, and swiveled on his right foot counter-clockwise back toward the slicer. As he turned, he passed a load-bearing metal pole of Fire Station proportions. It was painted white, and bore orange/purple stickers, one of which read 'SAUCY DOGS--$999/lb.'

He opened the Hubert's hand guard and placed the chicken in position. Pressed the big START button. The circular blade whirred.

"How'd you like that sliced?" Johnny gave what looked to be a thrilled smile.

"Not too thick's good."

"You got it." Johnny cranked the slicer knob a couple degrees, and slid off a quick one. He extended his hand, with the blazing orange meat contained, and said, "Try that on for size."

The man reached his right hand forward, stretching light brown fabric over a glass-enclosed case filled with cheeses, hams, breasts, and beef ready to be sliced into fresh cold cuts, like the one he presently received in his open palm. For a moment, Johnny's gloved fingertips touched the man's flesh from above, as gravity took its course.

The guy's paw closed around the slice.

He pulled it back to his jaws. Once it was three inches away, he parted his lips and revealed two rows of pearly yellows. By the time his mouth had opened, the chicken was inside.

He chewed and chewed and chewed, making squishy sounds. His countenance softened. He bent his knees a bit and his upper torso rocked back and forth.

"Whoa," he said, smiling, half a mouthful left. "That *is* Buck Wild!"

"Isn't it? And no nitrates."

"Well yea that's good too. Hey, I'll tell ya what. it's on like *no* backward for a full pound."

"OOOOOOOOOHHHHHHHH!" said A.J. fresh on the scene. He swiveled to face the customer. "I cannot believe you just said that!"

The man gave A.J. a U-shaped smile and put his hands down by his sides.

As Johnny slid the poultry back and forth against the cold metal of the machine, slices came out under the blade. He caught each as it emerged, and made a neat stack to three inches' height onto a piece of wax paper.

A.J. asked, "Do you feel like having everything and nothing would be good if we had access to everything in the world?"

"Having everything and nothing? Well, what do you mean by that, A.J?"

said Johnny.

A.J, cleaning the back Deli case, turned—bared his glazy eyes. His gothic disposition was augmented by a silvery chain with a gargoyle and rhinestone ruby pendant. Black and blue tye-dye tee shirt underneath.

"When we go into the place without fury, we keep it moving and have lots of time," he snarled.

"Whoa, hey, alright there Sailor," said Johnny in reply, giving a jolly side-to-side gesture and a closed-mouth smile, then an open one. His left hand enveloped the wax paper around the chicken, scooped it up, and placed it on the scale.

"It's a little under, is that okay?"

The man saw 0.96. He gave a smug smile and a thumbs up.

Johnny made a few keys beep, and out came a ticket with creaky grinding printer grunts, as each line of ink was transferred.

"Who *are* you?" asked A.J. to the 'on/no backward' guy.

"Just a guy who loves his meat," smiled the fella.

"Love on, my man. Love on," said A.J., now doing nothing in particular.

"Anything else I can getcha?" asked Johnny.

"Yeah, lemme grab a half pound of that Spring Slaw. So light and fluffy."

12.

"It's 11:17. I get a break soon," said A.J. to Francis. "You'll have to go later."

"Hey," said Steve, emerging forth from the Deli back room. "What's up with customers saying, 'Don't slice it *too thick*. When would someone ever ask for something sliced *too thick*?"

Francis burst out cackling.

Johnny jumped in, "Yeah, could you cut that a little *too thick* please?"

"Or, can I have a little 'too much'?" quipped A.J.

"Right."

"That's because when you ask customers how much they want, sometimes before they give a real answer, they say, 'Not too much.' Customers are dumb."

"Hey now," said Steve, "Most customers are very intelligent. Aren't you a customer when you go into other stores?"

"Oh!!! True that. It's on like 'no' backward!" said A.J.

"Heard that one," chimed Shigby.

13.

"You can tell me anything you want," A.J. said to the approaching blonde. She looked fit and healthy.

"Is this the Deli?" said the blonde. "I saw those cheeses and thought 'this must be the World Foods section.'"

"Nope. Other side of the store, after the bank, before the café."

"Ooh, there's a café?"

"That's right. Here, I'll show you." A.J. stepped out of the line.

The vixen held up a 'stop sign' hand and said, "I'm all set. Have a good one." And with a smile, *se fue*.

"Poof. Blond begone," mused A.J.

"She didn't seem like the Deli type," said Shigby.

14.

"No need to get too shifty with it," said A.J. to Francis, who was wriggling all over the slicer.

"Hey," said Shigby. "Do you guys believe the little things matter in life?"

"Do the little things matter…" echoed Johnny under his breath.

"In life," trailed off A.J., completing the round.

Francis played percussion on the steely meat machine.

"Yes, Shigby," said Johnny. "I do believe the little things matter. Why do you ask?"

"I see us all doing little things, and maybe they all add up."

"Little things are really important," said Francis.

A lady and her daughter approached the counter. The girl was skinny with black hair under hat, a blue poofy jacket, no hood, about four feet tall.
Mom was donning a tan trenchcoat and an orange floral/paisley scarf.

Golden Girl, like Lily.

"Hi there," said Francis.

"Stepping up to the plate," said Johnny.

"But he didn't clean off the slicer from his last customer."

"No-body's per-fect, A.J. Stop being so negative." said Shigby.

"Hello!" said the mom. "May I get a quarter pound of Hog's Face Sopresata?"

Francis quivered and touched the non-latex surface of his glove to his hat.

"No touching your head or face!" admonished A.J.

Francis looked at him. "What is sopresata?"

"It's a kind of meat. Made from a piggy. In Italy. You like piggies?" asked A.J.

Francis licked his lips. "Mmm…" he said. "I like livers. Any animal."

"You're a weird dude," said A.J. "I'm taking my break."

"Would you mind changing your gloves first?" The lady smiled sweetly as she asked.

"Before I take my break?" retorted A.J.

The lady's smile sank. "I was addressing your colleague."

"Sorry. Sopresata's out back. Shigby, keep an eye on Francis." With that, A.J. was gone.

"Sure!" said Francis. He changed his gloves and went out to the cheese and specialty rack. Steve was there, with his label gun.

"Which one is the…"

"Sopresata? I could hear you guys." Steve came over and handed Francis a piece that looked like a segment of arm, dark burgundy with pocked inlays of white fat. And pepper corns to spice up the already salty, smooth log.

"Thanks," said Francis, grabbing the meat. He walked out front, over to the counter.

"How would you like that sliced?" asked Francis.

"Thin."

"Okay." Francis put the slab on there and closed the guard. He pressed the ON button, adjusted the knob, and a-waaaaaaaaaay he went!

He sliced one. Held it up. "How's this look?"

"Good."

He held it out. "Would you like to have the sample?"

She took it in her hand and smiled. "Sure." She bit off about a third of it and radiated that 'Melt in your mouth' vibe. Teeth noshing, saliva digesting.

"Make that a half pound," she cooed.

"Okay," said Francis, who had already blasted out two slices.

Shigby, standing by, slurred, "You're good at this. I think you'll be alright."

"Th-th-thanks," said Francis.

They shared a mutually uncomfortable and mildly pleasurable moment.

Francis stacked a pile of salty red pork about two inches high. He dished it up onto the scale, .43 lbs. Back down.

Seven more slices later: .51. Job done.

"That's a wrap." Bagged it, tagged it, handed it to the lady—the girl was munching on the remainder of mom's slice.

"Have a great day," the little girl said.

"You too!" Francis gave an elbow wave.

After they had gone, Francis added, "The customers are nice."

"A lot of them arrrrrre," said Shigby. He took a brick of white American cheese and wrapped it in plastic. "I'm an excellent wrapper," he said.

"Heh. Do you play line rider?" asked Francis.

"Noooo. My feet hurt. Is that for the computerrrrs?"

"Yeah! You make a track and you ride on it, and you can do flips, and…"

"Hey guys!" interrupted a fella. "Could I get a quarter pound of Hog's Face turkey?"

"Sure. Oven roasted?"

"Yeppers!"

Shigby got it, sliced a sample. "How's this?" he asked, elevating the morsel.

"Good!" The young man extended his hand. Shigby gave.

The fella munched. "Not bad, not bad."

Shigby sliced thrice, picked up, turned around and weighed. There it was. 0.24.

"Nice job," said the gent.

As he was walking away, he said, "May the Star People bless you." And, clutching his breast, he shuffled toward checkout.

15.

At 11:30 Johnny said, "Ready to go on break?"

Francis answered, "Yep! I'll, ah, grab my lunch." He went to the closet and returned with a huge brown paper grocery bag.

Shigby muttered, "A.J. had better come back soon."

"Alright, you came prepared," said Johnny, eying Francis' grocery bag, and then waving to a returning Lily and Gran. "You'll be with me for the first fifteen. When you work heftier days, like 7 hours, you get a half hour, or two fifteens, but that's all work stuff. Tell me about you! What floats your boat, dude?"

They walked into the supermarket, toward the back, through Produce.

"I'm... into reading, and computers."

"Nice! Gamer? Or programmer. Or... other?"

"Gamer."

"Knew it! I have a few friends who play RPGs and you actually remind me of them, believe it or not."

"What kind of RPGs?"

"Let's see... D&D, Dominion..."

"Dominion is technically a deck-building card game." Francis knocked a bag of pistachios off a corner display with his elbow. He recoiled, flinched, gasped, then squatted down to pick it up. Once on the floor, he noticed a sticker on the ground.

He scraped rapidly at it with his thumbnail until Johnny said, "They'll take care of that during the night shift." As Francis got up and put the pistachios back, Johnny turned to him and whispered, "They won't take care of it."

Francis kinda smiled, and put his hands where his pockets would have been, were he not wearing pocketless jeans.

"Are you a runner?" asked Johnny.

"No. I hate the sunlight," said Francis.

"It can be bright," said Johnny, taking a left into the Grocery back room. He pushed open the double doors, held one for Francis, and walked past the Grocery office toward the punch clock.

He swiped his card, pushed a few buttons, and was on his way.

"Do I have to slide my card?"

"Good question. Not for short breaks, just lunch. What games are you into?" asked Johnny.

"I play one called Quargabuzz."

"Quargabuzz?"

They walked down the back hall to Dairy, then took a right, and hit up the stairs.

"It's a community of duck aliens. We get together and do adventurous rituals."

"My kind of party!" said Johnny.

As they reached the top, Johnny observed that Francis was less jittery than in the morning.

They sat down. Johnny grabbed a homemade egg salad sandwich and an organic gala apple out of his apron pocket.

Francis unsheathed a huge bag of cheddar and sour cream potato chips, a can of tuna, and a bottle of prune juice.

"Cheers," said Johnny.

"Cheers!" said Francis.

"So, you remember when I made Lily touch her head earlier?" asked Johnny.

"Yeah! That was awesome."

"Would you like to learn some more stuff like that? I guarantee A.J. won't teach this to you."

"Sure!"

"Okay. One thing you can do is called 'pacing.' That's when you match the rhythm of the person's speech or body language. If your customer... is talking... like this... then you... can talk... like this... also."

"Oh!"

"But if they have an extreme voice, like they talk really fast and high pitched, then you don't want to match them exactly. Instead, you can do about halfway between where you are and where they are."

"Okay."

"Actually I think that is called matching. No big deal. These terms all overlap. For pacing, if they talk... with this... rhythm, then you can tap your hand... with the same... rhythm. It's important to really connect with the people, though, and not think too much about techniques while you're dealing with them. Otherwise it'll seem fake and will hurt rapport."

"I might have to try that. Why don't you do something where you can use that, and make more money than at the Deli?"

"You know," said Johnny. "I just might."

They passed the remainder of Francis' fifteen minutes in conversation, and then a solitary Johnny relaxed and vegged out, until...

16.

At noon, he was back on the line.

"Much love and respect to all the people who made this possible!"

In his hands: two empty Chix Delish racks, having once held ten Chix.

"People were coming by, giving you kudos," said Shigby.

"Kudos the candy bar or kudos as in props?" asked Johnny with 'fake-puzzled' body language.

"Props, homie," said Shigby.

"Better make some more. My lady arriveth at 1:00."

"Who's your lady?" asked Shigby.

"Someone who needs to change her tune. She's got the communication making negative sensations. I'm here to give her the good vibrations."

"Well, alright there, Johnny," said Lily. "Thanks for the rap. I don't think she's negative, though. I get her emails, and they're pretty good. She brings up a lot of issues women are afraid to talk about, 'cuz men won't let 'em!" She winked and added, "You got me for another hour, so if you want to do the song again, say the word."

Johnny smiled. "My faithful sidekick." He stepped out back to the freezer and resumed presence a minute later, Chix Delish works in hand.

In ten minutes, the hot case was ready and willing for more Chix customers. Still plenty of Zingers, Dingers, fried chicken, and Chicken Pops.

"Sing with me?" said Johnny.

"Maybe once more this afternoon. I'm good for now," said Lily.

"Yeah you are," said Johnny. "But sing with me anyway."

"Alright." They went back and did it.

"Time to get your bearings on the platter," said Lily. "It's not gettin' any earlier."

Johnny nodded and went forth. The back room cutting board was clear, save the gnocchi. He pushed open the walk in door, and passed through that room. Exiting on the other side, he dodged a roast-beef-slicing Shigby. "Right behind ya, bub," said Johnny as he passed.

Shigby held up a slab of bloody red meat and asked, "How's this look?" to a three-and-a-half foot tall female, normally proportioned to her age.

"Good," she said as Johnny disappeared into the closet.

He grabbed a brown cardboard box bottom, and a fancy white and orange waxy cardboard top. Took a big metal tray, two feet in diameter, and a plastic lid to fit it.

With that, it was platter time. He walked straight across the Deli line, past the hand washing sink, the well-kept picture of Steve, and into the back room.

He put the metal platter tray down on the cutting board, and the lid on top. Placing the white and orange waxed cardboard top aside, he assembled the brown box bottom into a fine square structure. Then he put together the top.

"Twelve ten. Yikes." Johnny poked his head around the corner. "Gran, if you want to cut some meat for this platter, in fact that would be most helpful."

"Sorry got backed up," said Gran.

"Oh, indeed you are," said Johnny. Gran had a line three people deep. "My b, yo!" He turned around. "Guess it's on me to prep this platter."

He looked over by the phone, and found a clipboard. Picked it up, and read from the first page. "Ms. Migdonahan. Tharrr she blows."

"Is that the platter for the Drone?" asked Lily as she came out to the back room.

"Yeppp..."

"It's easy. Two pounds each of roast beef, oven baked turkey, and mortadella. And celery in the middle."

"Yee-haw."

"So what's the big deal? Why are you so jacked up about doing her platter?"

"Let's just say, I'm in a unique position to help her."

"With what? Johnny, you never talk like this. You're freakin' my freak, buddy."

"It's... complicated. Good job on the jingle today. You rocked it, girl."

"Thanks." She blushed. "You weren't too bad yourself. We're gonna need some more sandwiches though."

"Okay there Blanchita."

"Are you calling me Blanche again?"

"You gonna slice me the meat for that platter?"

"Ha ha. No. You on it?"

"Sure! Hey wait, your shoulder! You're not supposed to slice anyway."

"That's true. Thanks for the reminder." Lily smiled and turned the corner.

"Alright," said Johnny. "Two pounds of roast beef, turkey, and mort."

"You can do it," said Lily, washing her hands.

"Thank you. Platters are not my, how you say, *forte*. I'll put some extra magic in it."

Johnny went around front to the Deli and assessed the roast beef situation. Hog's Face, *thee* brand for platters, was running low, only a half pound end. "Not gonna cut it," he said.

"What's not gonna cut it," sneered A.J.

"Thissah roast beef, I needs abouts two poundsah for a plattah."

"I have the store brand over on the roast beef slicer. Use that." A.J. exhaled tobacco-smoke breath into Johnny's nostrils.

Francis watched on.

"I would," said Johnny, "But this is for a platter. And, as you know, we always use Hog's Face brand meats for Deli platters. Any idea why that is, Francis?"

"Because it's more expensive?" Francis took a guess.

"Bingo!" said A.J. "I like this guy."

"And it's higher quality, no preservatives, no nitrates, the roast beef is lower sodium..."

When Francis had turned away to help a customer, A.J. growled, "Don't ever upstage me in front of a new hire." His voice was low and cruel.

"Why... so... serious!!?" asked Johnny. "I was providing information, A.J. Come on, buddy. Nothing personal."

"Sorry," said A.J. "I've been sniffing a lot of pixie powder lately."

"Pixie powder?"

A new customer, a forty-some-odd stout fella wearing overalls and a Red Sox cap, looked on, waiting.

"Blow."

"Um... hey mind serving this fellow? I gotta hit the platter hard. Thanks bro. Let's talk later."

"Right." said A.J. looking down, then askance at the man. "Can I help you sir?"

"Excuse me, I was next," said a woman in the amassing crowd.

Off Johnny went to open a fresh Hog's Face roast beef. He picked it up off the shelf with both hands. He walked into the Deli back room by opening the door with his shoulder. There, he made his way to the sinks and grabbed a large knife.

"I'm opening up the Hog's Face," he said.

"Make sure the Hog's cheeks don't fall out," croaked a passing Shigby.

Johnny held the beef a safe distance from his body, with his left hand. He sliced the loaf with the point and first two inches of the knife. A reddish-clear liquid gushed through the slit in the plastic, and more when he removed the blade.

Set the knife down on the counter. Turned on the water. Cleaned the metal, and put it back on the wall, with the other cutting instruments.

Stripped the rest of the meat of its plastic.

Kept it working forth toward the Deli slicers.

A.J. scolded, "I told you to use the generic stuff!"

"Bro, give it a rest, wouldja? You know I respect you, but come on now, let's keep it kosher."

Johnny put the roast beef in spinning blade's way, and began producing cross sections.

A pound later, Johnny was ready to do another. After that, he was done. He weighed out the grand total: two pounds.

He turned off the slicer, pulled back the tray, opened the handle, and removed the roast beef. He brought it back to the meat storage case and wrapped it up on the cutting board.

"I'm an excellent wrapper," said Johnny.

"Hey, that's... my... line." said Shibgy. "I can wrap with the best of 'em."

"Yes, you are also a mad phat wrapper," said Johnny.

"Oven roasted... there 'tis." Johnny reached for it, and... got it! A nice big breast. No need to run out back for the turkey.

He wiped down the middle slicer for this one.

The slap of meat on metal.

Another two pounds, next to the roast beef. Four lbs on the scale all together.

Johnny wrapped up the turkey, put it back, and grabbed the mortadella he had been gifted from the Creator.

Whammo. Two pounds later, and he was "Ready to plat the platter!"

He turned off, cleaned up, wrapped, put away. Took six pounds of meat to the Deli back room. "She doesn't like cheese?" he called to Lily.

"No. She's lactose intolerant."

"What about Swiss?"

"No cheese. Never has, never will."

"Alrighty. Platting!"

"Hey some of your chickens are almost done."

"Was thinking that... want to take them down for me? Ha ha..."

"Yeah, you wish buddy. Come out when you can."

"Hokay dokay." Johnny put the platter meats down in back, on the cutting board.

He strutted out front to see three spits of blackened chicken on the right, and three spits warmed up but not done, on the left.

"Oh-kay... you meant it when you said the chickens were getting done."

"You ah coh-rrect," said Lily.

Johnny tossed nine stacked rotisserie chicken containers—tops and bottoms—in a row on the counter, and dropped in diapers to boot.

He printed three 'Original' price labels and stuck them on his arms.

"Hey chicken guy," said a Seafood lady.

"Heyyy..." said Johnny flirtatiously, waving his sticker-clad arms.

Johnny opened the oven and pulled out the top chickens. Sizzling. As an afterthought, he stuck in the thermometer. "As expected. 182. Done."

With one stroke, he picked up the pliers, removed the first spider, and lifted the spit at an angle so all three chickens slid off.

In under five seconds, the chicks were transferred to three vacant containers, diapers notwithstanding.

On snapped the lids, then *swoosh!* went the price labels. The cardboard sleeves with their handles, the ornamental flavor stickers... and *voila*. All on. Over to the hot case.

As he repeated, he asked Lily, "What's new with dancing? You been out lately?"

"Yeah, I have, funny you should mention that," said Lily. "A few girlfriends and I went out on the town recently. And there was this other girl dancing there, but not with us... we were all getting down, having a good time, you know? So we're all dancing, and the end of the night comes. She walks over to us and says, 'Hey had a great time dancing with you.' Thought it was kinda funny."

"That she would say she had a great time dancing with you."

"Yeah! What you don't?"

"So you didn't actually dance with her, face to face?"

"No, that's what I'm saying!"

"Ahh... How do you *feel* about that?"

"Johnny... come on."

"Wait, what am I coming on?"

Lily hit his arm.

Shigby announced, "I'm taking a break."

Francis and Steve were working the Deli counter. A.J. was nowhere to be seen. Gran was out back filling the Spring Slaw.

"Have fun, Shigs." Johnny closed these three lids, put on the stickers, packed them up, and brought them to the hot case.

Next, he printed three labels for Honey Gold flavor rotisserie chickens. Stuck those on his right arm.

Johnny turned around and lifted the bottom spit off the oven. Unloaded it —had the meat off the spit before it even hit the baking sheet. Each chicken practically flew into its corresponding receptacle.

Those, and lastly, three Whiskey flavored, whole Rotisserie chickens, journeyed it into the hot case.

"*Bon voyage*, chickies. Best wishes, and may your clucks ring for eternity."

"You are a funny fella," said Lily.

"Just noticing this now?" asked Johnny. "Come on!"

"Ohp, twelve thirty five, you'd better finish your platter!"

Johnny closed the oven, chucked his gloves, and put on new ones.

He grabbed some fancy toothpicks. "She likes the plain ones," said Lily. "And no olives. Just the meat, folded real pretty."

"Got it." Johnny remembered the lady's raspy voice on the phone, ordering him to hold the fancy stuff.

He put the color-flagged toothpicks back and picked up the straight light brown ones.

Carried them to the Deli back room. Starting with the roast beef, he laid out each meat slice, in a curled fashion, so the entire arrangement came out looking like the frills of a clown's collar. Going clockwise after the beef was turkey, which he had sliced thin enough to curl and make palatable to the eye. Lastly, he placed the ham in the triune meat presentation. All in all, a meal fit for an army.

"Best presented with some kind of bread, no?"

"She just wants the meat, I'm tellin' ya," said Lily.

Johnny tagged the platter. Then Steve came around the corner with Francis and said, "Johnny you mind helping out at the Deli while I get Francis into the system upstairs?"

"You got it, boss!"

17.

Johnny gave the lady a thumbs up sign. Every time she looked at him, he smiled a little bit. His eyes were about two-thirds of the way open, and they twinkled.

"So, what do you do when you're not working at the Deli?" the woman asked.

"I have some hobbies, good natured things."

"Such as…"

"Fishing, throwing get-togethers, parties if you will…"

"What kind of get-togethers do you throw? What do you do there?"

"We play darts, drink, play video games, have a good time."

Behind the woman, a guy with black curly hair, and a black V-neck cardigan sweater stood and glared. "Come on, buddy, this isn't social hour."

"Yessir," said Johnny.

The lady froze up like a cat arching her back. After she had softened, she said, "Well that was rude."

"You wanted half a pound miss?"

"Yes *sir*," she replied, with a smile at Johnny, then a sideways glance at the dude behind her.

Johnny placed the turkey breast on the slicer and got to moving it back and forth.

"What's your problem?" said the lady to the guy.

"I don't have a problem, you were taking a long time."

"Sir, are you feeling left out?" asked Johnny. He finished the final stroke, and put the bundle on the scale. "Point four six."

"One more slice, please," said the lady. Johnny nodded.

"Is anyone else pretending to work back there?" asked the guy.

"Haha, good one sir. Now that you mention it, there is someone who could be out here. At least I think that's the case."

He slapped on the slice, pressed the product number, and hit PRINT. Bagged that puppy up, and handed it to the lady.

"I'd like a few more items," said the lady.

"Absolutely, ma'am, I shall get my esteemed colleague and then serve you."

Johnny elbowed the gray double doors open, keeping his hands visible. "Hey, A.J., mind helping up front for a minute?"

"Sure!" came a voice from the depths of the walk in. "What's the deal, kid?" now louder as he emerged folding a piece of paper and gave his side-to-side smile sneer. "Can I help who's next?"

He pocketed a pen and looked out at the crowd.

"Fifteen minutes, J-man!" shouted Lily while the curly-haired guy ordered a pound and a quarter of Cajun style turkey from A.J.

"Lily, thank you. You are on point," Johnny said to his sidekick.

Alright. Let's get to it," said Johnny. "What can I grab for ya."

The lady smiled and held up a Post-it sized piece of paper. "Three pounds of liverwurst, sliced thin," and her expression broke. She cackled, "Just kidding. Three Kraben beef franks would be outstanding."

"Ha ha excellent, *Madame*." Johnny swooped down on the hot dogs, with tongs. He put three into a bag, and onto the scale. Punched in the code, and the number 3, then PRINT.

"A half pound of egg salad," said the lady, with an upward inflection.

Executed.

"Two thirds of a pound of Little Red potato salad"—upward again.

Scoop, slap, done. A.J. was slicing next to him.

Meanwhile, two new customers had emerged and were standing behind the lady and the guy. The nubs looked Euro, with slicked-back dews and sewn coat pockets. And those jeans that look like they've been through a war but only cost $500.

"And three quarters of a pound of honey ham, shaved. I'm serious this time."

"You got it."

As Johnny went for the ham, A.J. weighed and printed one and a quarter pound of Cajun.

The two Euros spoke to each other in some Germanic language and pointed up to the board.

Johnny heard A.J. say, "I stayed up all last night, so I'm a little out of it."

He looked up and the number of customers waiting had doubled. Two soccer moms, their kids, and a black guy had just shown up.

"I'm going to college. This job is temporary. I wouldn't be working here if I had a choice."

The black guy spoke to A.J. "Hey, can we get some cheese with that whine?"

One of the soccer moms laughed.

"Ha ha, very funny," said A.J. "Where is Shigby?"

"He's on break."

"For a half hour? What the..."

"It hasn't been that long."

Johnny's customer asked for a pound of liverwurst, all in one chunk.

"Yes'm," said Johnny.

Once he had sliced and delivered, the lady said, "Thank you," and left.

"Number 121," said Johnny. One of the soccer moms stepped up.

Before Johnny's wurst customer was out of sight, A.J. said, "What a jerk. She asked for liverwurst, said she was joking, then ordered a million other things, then asked for liverwurst in real life."

"Yeah," said A.J.'s customer, the white guy with black hair. "I was ready to give her a tongue lashing."

The soccer mom who had laughed, walked away in the direction of the lady Johnny had been serving.

The other soccer mom, #121, looked up at Johnny then down at the cold salads.

"Is there a difference between the Spring Slaw and the store brand slaw?" she asked.

A family of three joined the crowd. The boy and girl fought over who would push the ticket button while their dad looked on.

"Yep, the Spring Slaw tastes amazing," said Johnny. "And we make it fresh in the Deli, every day."

"Ooh, that does sound good," said the soccer mom. "I'll take a pound."

"You got it."

"Johnny, I gotta go in five minutes, bud. It's 12:55."

"No prob, Lily." Johnny slapped on new gloves and picked up a 16-ounce container.

As he was about to slide open the cold case window, the liverwurst lady stormed the Deli with a female store manager, and a soccer mom.

"That's him!" she said, pointing at A.J.

The store manager rolled up her starched pink shirt sleeves and glared. "A.J., did you talk badly about this woman?"

A.J. looked up with surprise, as if asked whether he had committed murder. "Marla, no!" he exclaimed.

"I heard him," said the soccer mom.

"I did too," said the guy with black curly hair.

A.J. glanced at him with panic. "What the heck, man!?"

"A.J., you're fired," said Marla.

"WHAT!?? I'm your best worker!"

Johnny smiled as he scooped Spring Slaw.

"Alright. Well, I'm not going to do what everyone thinks I'm gonna do, and FREAK OUT!" A.J. flailed his arms and bobbed his head. "But what I do want to know is..."

"Can it. Gather your belongs and leave the property, now."

"Who's coming with me?" A.J. put out his hands, palms up, and waved his fingers.

Silence.

"Who's coming with me?"

Silence.

"FINE! Screw you people! I'm outta here." A.J. stomped off the line, into the supermarket.

Lily grabbed her purse and walked out of Prep.

A.J. whirled around with a gleam in his eye. "Lily, you're coming with me?"

"No, I'm done with my shift. Come back and say hi!"

A.J. yelled, "I'm getting paid for this whole day!"

Marla sighed and said, "You worked until 1. I'll clock you out. Come back Friday for your check."

A.J. fizzled and fumed out the 'In' door, and he was gone.

18.

Amidst the commotion, a pair of gnarled feet, in once pretty, but now ragged shoes, shuffled their way past the cash registers. The adjoined body was tilted forward so that if it contained a heart, the ever-loving blood-pumping organ was pointed to the floor.

The form resembled a masculine femaleness. The clothes were ladyish— a long, worn black dress and conservative floral blouse.

Her head shook with each lurch forward. She held her arms tight, pressed against her sides, like a T-Rex.

"The Drone," said Johnny under his breath. He could swear he smelled mothballs. Louder, he said to Marla, "I need to take care of this platter. Any idea where Steve and Francis are?"

"They're right here," said Marla.

Around the corner, Francis and Steve were smiling and laughing. Steve looked up and saw the crowd, and said, "Johnny, we'll take the line. Your lady awaits."

"EXCUSE ME!" A gnarled head spewed rage across the soup station.

"Yes, ma'am!" said Johnny. "Ms. Migdonahan, I presume?"

The lady's expression became neutral—an average between her previous venom and Johnny's joy.

"Yes, it is I."

"So glad you are here. I will grab your platter for you."

"Thank—thank you," said the Drone while Johnny disappeared around the corner.

He was back in a flash, carrying a big box around the front, to her cart.

"This might sound strange, but I'm a big fan of your blog," said Johnny.

"Get out!" said the Drone. Her face lit up like a schoolgirl's. "But you're a..."

"A man, yes it's true. But *you* know, when people *love* what they do, they *men*-tion things that other people can understand, regardless of who they are, or what they believe."

Ms. Migdonahan appeared 30 years younger. She stood upright, and her shoulders relaxed and spread out, so there was space under her armpits.

"I..." she was interrupted by a loud, young male voice.

"I came back to get my hoodie. Now I'm gone. Are you the Drone? Bite me, you negative whore."

As A.J. was beginning to walk away, Johnny grabbed him by the collar. "A.J., you have disrespected not only this woman, but yourself, and everyone in here. Apologize at once."

Ms. Migdonahan watched on in fascination.

At first A.J. tensed up as if he would hit J. Then he relaxed, turned to the Drone, and said, "I'm sorry ma'am, I have been having a bad day."

"You look like you've been having a bad life," said the Drone. She and Johnny cackled and chuckled uproariously.

"Ha ha..." A.J. slumped his shoulders. "Alright, bye guys. I'll stop by and say wassup."

With that, he was out the door.

"This is about the most fun I've had in years," said the Drone. "I don't know how you did it, but you've changed my outlook, young man."

"Well, *I* know *love* and happiness can find *you* when you least expect it," said Johnny.

"If you'll excuse me," said Ms. Migdonahan at a rapid clip, "You just gave me a blog post idea."

"Go get 'em!" said Johnny. "May you flourish with ever greater abundance."

They locked eyes, and the world changed.

As she floated away, onlookers scarcely recognized her as the same creature who had hobbled in.

The last customers of the rush walked off, provisions in tow. Steve and Francis had whittled the line down to two college-slacker-looking gents.

Gran walked up to Johnny from the cheese station and smiled. "You're amazing," she said. "I always wanted to see her smile, and lighten up. She's a different person than when she came in her, thanks to you."

Shigby waddled around the corner, carrying a jar of pickles. He grunted, "Did I miss anything? My feet hurt."

19.

Now that it was quiet, Johnny turned his attention to the hot case. "Not much going on. Almost out of Chix Delish, need Dingers, Zingers, and..."

"And your chickens are done," said Carl.

"Right—I'll serve up the Chix then get to unspittin'."

"You're the best, kid."

"Hey, why are you being so nice?" asked Johnny.

Carl smiled. "I saw what you did with that lady. ***You... love... men.*** I know about those mind tricks. How do you think I get so many loyal Seafood customers? She's a tough cookie. I've known her for years."

"Just doing my job," Johnny said with a wink.

Around the corner, in the back room, Steve hoisted a palate-shaped box onto the counter next to the sink. "I'm stickin' chicks," he said. "Francis and Shigby should be okay out there, Gran's on Cheese, and we got a couple kids coming in at 2. Do you want to clock out early?"

"Sure!" Johnny said, and then queried, "Is 2 okay? That'll give me 45 minutes to finish the Chix Delish, pull down the rotisserie chickens, and cook up some Dingers, Zingers, and maybe some fried chicken."

"Sure, bud. Thanks for your work."

Johnny walked back to the freezer and pulled one bag of each—Regular and Spicy Chix Delish.

Out front, he checked for buns.

A few bags. He dropped six original breast filets into the fryer basket and lowered it. Set the timer for five minutes.

He spread out ten buns on the long cutting board where Lily had been working. Over at the scale, he printed ten labels—six Regular and four Spicy.

Shigby and Francis were serving a short line of people. Every so often Francis asked about an item, and Shigby replied with a drippy, helpful answer.

Johnny sprayed each bun with Butter Buds.

The fryer beeped and Johnny pulled the Chix. He tossed them to the left, into a black plastic full pan, lined with parchment paper.

In one fluid motion, he dumped four Spicy Chix, dropped them in the oil, set the timer for 5, and changed his gloves.

Johnny brought the pan over to Lily's cutting board and placed each Chix on a buttery bun. He put on the tops, making six closed-face sandwiches. Took bags from below, for Regular and Spicy, and placed them on the counter.

Into six bags went six Chix Delish sandwiches. He filled an empty rack in in the hot case, just in time for the buzzer.

Four Spicy Chix later, Johnny was ready for the other fried goods and the Rot Chx.

And the details of how Johnny prepared four bags of Dingers, three bags of Zingers, an eight-piece and a four piece fried chicken—all while pumping out three spits of Original, Honey, and Whiskey flavored rotisserie chicken—need they be detailed? Suffice it to say that it all took 30 minutes.

At 1:50, Lily rushed to the Deli in her street clothes—jeans and a purple and pink rocker tee. "Johnny! Gran! Guys!" she breathed.

"What!" exclaimed Johnny.

"You're not going to believe this. The Drone just updated her blog. Look at this: 'All Men Are NOT Scum'!"

Lily was waving around her Smart phone like an Olympic torch.

Gran looked up from wrapping a Swiss cheese loaf. "She has a new article?"

"Listen—'I had the pleasure of being defended by a young man at the Come & Buy grocery store today. It changed my point of view in a way I cannot describe—but one thing I know. The problem is not men—at least not all of them. The problem is...' and then she goes onto a bunch of negative stuff. But Johnny, she sounds like a different person!"

Johnny smiled. "It's the little things, isn't it?"

"I was hoping she'd see the bright side," said Gran with a twinkle. "Good for her."

"Well, I guess I'll call it a day." Johnny took off his gloves and stepped away from the line. "Gran you're clocking out too, right?"

"In a minute, want to finish up here. See you soon, my friend."

"Y'all have a great one. Nice job—actually, super job, Francis. You rock, buddy. Happy to have you here."

"Thanks!" said Francis.

Lily was staring at Johnny.

"Yes?"

"Johnny, I have to know. What did you do, with the Drone?"

"Huuuuh?" Johnny put a bottle of pickles on the counter and looked at Lily.

"I know you did your hypnosis stuff, at least I figure you did... like when you made me scratch my nose..."

"You are a smart cookie," said Johnny, hand on the counter.

"But I feel like..." Lily twirled her finger in her hair, "there was something more going on."

"You really want to know?" Johnny's tone was soft.

"I... yeah."

"I entered her deep psyche."

"Why? How?" Lily's eyes darted back and forth as she softly asked.

Johnny looked over one shoulder, then the other. "Lily... this is serious." He paused, placed the pickles under the counter fridge. "I..." he made eye contact, "really trust you, and since you are her fan, it may be good to tell you. But it is secret, honestly."

Lily half-screwed-up her face—her eyes sparkled. "Okay... yeah. You can trust me. What's the secret?"

"This woman, the Drone. How many fans does she have?"

Lily looked down, paused, and then looked back. "Ten thousand plus, online."

"And growing."

"Ya... she's a celeb."

Johnny nodded. "And as her influence increases in number, it also increases in her readers' hearts."

"Aha."

"And you know what happens when someone has a hold of your heart. They possess your mind, and even your soul is changed."

"Oh..."

"The Drone, in possession of so many female souls, would cause their husbands and suitors such frustration that they would commit unthinkable acts against their fellows. The women who read her tend to date low-value men, who are already looking for a reason to snap."

Lily's eyes searched Johnny's face. He looked as one accurately reporting weighty information.

"You've thought about her quite a bit," said Lily.

"Yep. My... mentor and I have taken an interest in people like her, influential and negative. We've studied her growth. She was becoming big enough to blot out consciousness on a grand scale. Now she will raise and clear it. Or, more aptly..." Johnny watched Lily as he spoke... "We all will—and now she is a willing, positive participant."

"How long have you been planning this?" asked Lily, oblivious to the rest of the store, which, fortunately, was oblivious to her.

"Since I came here. All the studying was related to this day, so I could alchemize the *exact* vibe she needed me to carry."

"Huh. So... what did you do to get her to write that blog post? Did you tell her to?"

"She was inspired." Johnny grinned.

As Gian strolled by, smooth leather shoes clicking on the floor, Johnny said, "Well, I'd better wrap up and get heading..."

"Wait but..." Lily, mute, ogled Johnny's back.

He turned around. "You workin' tomorrow?"

"Yea."

"I am off, but I can tell you more if I come in to say 'Hi.'"

"Alright. Please do. All this is kind of a lot to take in." Lily tapped her pink fingernails on a stainless steel fixture.

"Remember our agreement. I trust you."

"You got it, bub. Jeez, Johnny. Freak me out sometimes! Byee!"

As Lily gathered herself, Johnny asked, "Hey. Why didn't you stay and see her?"

"I've met her. Her strength is so inspiring, but it can be a bit much in person."

"Yeah, she has a powerful vibe. Well, take care."

Lily smiled, shook her head, shouldered her purse, and walked off.

Gian swooped over from the specialty case.

"Telling stories are we?" he asked.

"Oh... what have you been up to, man?" returned Johnny, dodging the question.

Gian adjusted his tie. "Listening to you, and taking full responsibility."

"Wait." Johnny peered into Gian's face. "You... Crafty. Dog!"

"Yessir," Gian's accent morphed to 'Wild Wild West.'

"Why didn't I recognize you this morning!??"

"I had to hide myself, man, come on!"

"Well, OK! Makes sense."

"What's yer plan?"

"Get 'injured' tomorrow, come in, tell everyone I can't work, sorry, so long... say goodbye to Lily."

"Think she'll talk?"

"No, I trust her. It's between me, her, and *La Drone*."

"Gonna tell her where you're really from?"

"Doubtful. She wouldn't believe me anyway."

"Good insight. I'm proud of ya. Well, see you back in the city!" said Gian. "Oh, how do you like 'Gian', as a name?"

"Heh. Not bad. Anyone ask you about it?"

"Nobody."

"Your bro has some connections, man."

"Sure enough. Alright, Johnny, you take care now."

"Be blessed, Caesar."

"Be blessed. Love over power."

With that, Caesar walked on.

Johnny looked around—miraculously none of the others appeared to have noticed the intercourse.

"Shigby, Steve, Gran, Lily, Carl, Sushi..." Each waved or looked up and nodded. "Take good care, everybody."

"See ya, Johnny."

Johnny walked through Produce, said goodbye to Brent, and made his way to the Grocery back room.

When he got there, the Creator was sitting in the lotus position.

"It is finished," said Johnny.

"I am aware," said the Creator. "Caesar is pleased."

"True," said Johnny. "I'm glad he came. He is the most clever..."

"Intelligent."

"Intelligent person. Did you recognize him earlier?"

"Yes. I always do." The Creator's face glowed green. "Unless he uses fourth-fractal ether shrouds, but he did not today."

"I have so much to learn," said Johnny.

"Oh... what have you been up to, man?" returned Johnny, dodging the question.

Gian adjusted his tie. "Listening to you, and taking full responsibility."

"Wait." Johnny peered into Gian's face. "You... Crafty. Dog!"

"Yessir," Gian's accent morphed to 'Wild Wild West.'

"Why didn't I recognize you this morning!??"

"I had to hide myself, man, come on!"

"Well, OK! Makes sense."

"What's yer plan?"

"Get 'injured' tomorrow, come in, tell everyone I can't work, sorry, so long... say goodbye to Lily."

"Think she'll talk?"

"No, I trust her. It's between me, her, and *La Drone*."

"Gonna tell her where you're really from?"

"Doubtful. She wouldn't believe me anyway."

"Good insight. I'm proud of ya. Well, see you back in the city!" said Gian. "Oh, how do you like 'Gian', as a name?"

"Heh. Not bad. Anyone ask you about it?"

"Nobody."

"Your bro has some connections, man."

"Sure enough. Alright, Johnny, you take care now."

"Be blessed, Caesar."

"Be blessed. Love over power."

With that, Caesar walked on.

Johnny looked around—miraculously none of the others appeared to have noticed the intercourse.

"Shigby, Steve, Gran, Lily, Carl, Sushi..." Each waved or looked up and nodded. "Take good care, everybody."

"See ya, Johnny."

Johnny walked through Produce, said goodbye to Brent, and made his way to the Grocery back room.

When he got there, the Creator was sitting in the lotus position.

"It is finished," said Johnny.

"I am aware," said the Creator. "Caesar is pleased."

"True," said Johnny. "I'm glad he came. He is the most clever..."

"Intelligent."

"Intelligent person. Did you recognize him earlier?"

"Yes. I always do." The Creator's face glowed green. "Unless he uses fourth-fractal ether shrouds, but he did not today."

"I have so much to learn," said Johnny.

"And you shall," answered the Creator. "You shall."

"Hey," said Johnny. "Have you considered initiating Steve, for a pilgrimage?"

"I have." The Creator fell silent in that manner Johnny knew to restrict further flow on a subject.

"How long are you staying around? Cya tomorrow?"

"Tomorrow? What is that?" asked the Creator.

Both laughed.

"A little while—then I am back home."

"I'll be there, Sir. Like old times."

Mutual bows.

Johnny walked up to the punch clock and swiped his card.

The screen read 'TOO EARLY.'

"Oh, duh... may I use your card, Mastah Creator?"

The Creator produced a purple plastic rectangle, which Johnny swiped through the machine, followed by his own card.

The screen read '2:00 – ACCEPTED.'

ABOUT THE AUTHOR

Andrew Golay resides in temperate coastal regions. He has written two books, *707* and *Johnny Starks Deli Messiah*. To contact him, email andrew@andrewgolay.org. Your feedback and input (and readership!) are very appreciated.

Other than writing fiction, Golay enjoys the outdoors, studying and learning, exercise (jogging, yoga, qigong, dancing), and relationships with friends and family, including his awesome nephew and niece.

Made in the USA
Middletown, DE
20 May 2016